THE MAN WHO FOUI

Alexander Belyae

Translation and cover art by Maria K. with images provided by 123rr
Editing by Pubright Manuscript Services

EBOOK EDITION

*****

PUBLISHED BY:

TSK Group LLC

THE MAN WHO FOUND HIS FACE

Copyright © 2013 by TSK Group LLC

License Notes

All rights reserved. No portion of this book may be reproduced in any form without permission from the publisher, except as permitted by U.S. copyright law. For permissions contact: help@tskg.net.

TABLE OF CONTENTS

PART ONE 1
   A MINSTREL'S DRAMA *1*
   KILLING LAUGHTER *11*
   YOUR NOSE IS YOUR TREASURE *15*
   MAGICIAN ZORN *18*
   A NEW PATIENT *22*
   SETTLING IN *24*
   DON'T CHANGE YOUR FACE! *27*
   A DIFFICULT CASE *32*
   HORMONES AND GLANDS *39*
   SACRILEGE *45*
   THE MIRACLE OF TRANSFORMATION *49*
   PERPETRATOR *53*
   REJECTED AGAIN *57*
   IT'S OUR NOSE, NOT YOURS *62*
   EXPLOITING THE PAST FAME *66*
   BREAKING AND ENTERING *68*
   AN UNUSUAL TRIAL *71*
   A FAREWELL DINNER *75*
   VICTIMS OF "SORCERY" *79*
   MOUSETRAP *82*

PART TWO 86
   BY THE EMERALD LAKE *86*
   SCIENTIST RANGER *90*
   EUREKA *97*
   HOME AGAIN *113*
   THE NEW SANCHO PANZA *117*
   THE STRUGGLE BEGINS *123*
   THE LOST ADMIRER *126*
   ELLEN BEGINS A NEW LIFE *129*
   UNEXPECTED SUCCESS *133*
   PRESTO'S NEW FACE DEVELOPS *137*
   FAITHFUL FRIEND TO THE END *139*
   ORANGE BLOSSOMS *142*
   EXTRAS DOWNSTAGE *146*
   AN UNEXPECTED SETBACK *149*
   THE FATE OF THE FILM IS DECIDED *151*

TRIUMPH	*154*
IT'S HER…	*157*
THE FINAL STRIKE	*159*
ABOUT THE AUTHOR	**162**

THE MAN WHO FOUND HIS FACE

PART ONE

A MINSTREL'S DRAMA

Exhausted dogs were pulling a sled across a snow-covered plain. Their handler urged them on, but he too was stumbling from fatigue. A man in the sled lay unconscious, his head hanging helplessly off the edge. The handler fell. The dogs halted and sprawled in the snow.

There were cacti growing right next to the snowy expanse. A small man, almost a dwarf, was walking along the sidewalk shaded by chestnut trees. He was dressed in a tailored summer suit and a wide-brimmed panama hat. He couldn't help but see the drama in the snow, but passed by it indifferently.

The snow-covered plain ended. It was followed by an empty lot and then – a desert with palm trees and an oasis. Something dramatic was happening there as well. A Bedouin on horseback snatched up a beautiful girl in a European suit, threw her across his saddle and kicked his horse into a gallop. The girl screamed, reached out, and struggled. Several Europeans ran to their horses and gave chase.

The little man's eyes glided absentmindedly over the oasis, the Bedouin, and his pursuers. He kept walking, comically kicking up his feet.

The desert was followed by a pier. A large ocean liner was being loaded up. Steam rose from the four low smokestacks. A siren howled. There was a scuffle on the gangway. Someone was caught. Someone broke free and fell.

There was another empty lot. Mountains appeared. A medieval castle rose proudly, surrounded by walls and moats filled with water. A knight rode up a drawbridge leading to the castle and demanded the gates be opened. People were watching him from the walls. Suddenly, the bridge started rising. The knight's frightened horse panicked and tried to jump off the bridge.

Without waiting to see whether the horse jumped or ended up trapped along with its rider, the little man looked away and grumbled, looking obviously bored, "The same thing over and over. Boring!"

He kept walking down the smooth sidewalk.

Right next to him, along the paved road, flowed the endless stream of cars – white, navy, pale blue, golden like ground beetles, from the latest glossy limousines to the old worn-out Fords. People riding and cars and walking down the sidewalks treated the snow-covered plane, the oasis, the ocean liner, and the medieval castle with the same indifference as the little man.

They were much more interested in the man himself. Everyone walking and driving kept glancing at him. As soon as they saw him, people exchanged meaningful glances. Smiles appeared on their faces, accompanied by a kind of interest usually displayed by visitors to a zoo when they saw an exotic animal. At the same time, people did their best to treat the little man with respect. Acquaintances nudged each other and said quietly, "Look! Presto! Antonio Presto!"

"He weighs so little and is worth so much!"

"They say his capital is up to a hundred million dollars."

"Actually, it's over three hundred million."

"And he is still young, the lucky man!"

"Why is he not driving? He has one of the best cars in the world. It's custom made."

"This is his usual morning walk. The car is following him."

The little man continued walking, trying to blend in and attract no attention. However, he succeeded about as well as an elephant walking through a provincial village. Everything about him – his figure, his gestures, his facial expressions – was unusual. His every movement brought on a smile or a burst of laughter. He was the embodiment of all things funny. Even as a child he provoked laughter everywhere he went. He could be happy, sad, or pensive, he could be angry or indignant – but the result was always the same: people laughed. This irritated him at first, but later he became used to it. He had no choice. Such was his appearance.

He was almost a dwarf, had a very long torso, short legs, and the long arms of a normal grown-up man. Combined with his small height, his arms hung almost to his knees. His big head was wide at the top and narrow toward the bottom, having retained something childish in its structure. Particularly funny was his fleshy nose with its deep-seated bridge. The tip of the nose was pointed up, like a Turkish slipper. This nose was uncommonly agile, which caused not only the expression but the entire shape of the man's face to change every minute. Presto was a complete and authentic oddity, but there was nothing repulsive about his ugliness.

On the contrary, it was engaging. His big, lively, brown eyes shone with kindness and intelligence. He was truly an exceptional creation of nature.

Antonio Presto walked through the laughing crowd unperturbed, his short legs moving comically.

He turned left into a cypress alley leading into a large garden. In the garden, surrounded by eucalyptus trees, stood a Chinese gazebo. Presto entered and found himself in an elevator. An elevator in the middle of the garden may have surprised the uninformed, but Presto was very familiar with this strange structure. Nodding in response to the greeting from a boy manning the elevator, Presto ordered, "Down!"

He accompanied the statement with such an expressive gesture, as if he wanted to pierce the ground all the way to hell. It was so funny, that the boy started laughing. Presto gave him a menacing look. This only caused the boy to laugh louder.

"Pardon me, Mister, but I can't, I really can't..." The boy tried to apologize.

Presto sighed in defeat.

"It's alright, John, you don't have to apologize. It's no more your fault than it is mine. Is Mister Pitch here?" he asked.

"Twenty minutes ago."

"And Miss Gedda Lux?"

"Not yet."

"Of course," Presto said irately. His nose moved like a tiny elephant's trunk.

The boy once again couldn't help himself and squealed with laughter. It was just as well that the elevator halted, or else Presto would have gotten angry.

Antonio hopped out of the elevator, walked down a wide corridor, and found himself in a large round room lit with powerful lamps. After the already hot morning sun, the room was cool, and Presto sighed with relief. He quickly crossed the round room and opened the door into the adjacent space. It was as if a time machine transported him from the 20th century into medieval Germany.

A huge hall was before him, its ceiling culminating in a series of narrow arches. Doors, windows, and chairs were tall and narrow. Light fell through the windows, casting a sharply outlined shadow of the Gothic window pattern onto the wide stone tiles of the floor. Presto entered the beam of light and paused. Surrounded by all this tall and narrow furniture his form looked particularly small, awkward, and ridiculous. This was not an accident – this contrast was carefully planned by the director.

The old German castle was made of plywood, glue, canvas and paint based on the drawings, sketches and models of a famous architect who could build real castles and palaces, if he so wished. However, Mister Pitch, the owner of the film production company Pitch and Co, paid the architect a lot more than any aristocrat could ever offer for building real castles. And so the architect preferred to build movie sets from canvas and plywood.

There was a lot going on in the medieval castle, or rather, in the corner of the hall and behind its plywood walls. Workers, painters, artists, and carpenters, overseen by the architect himself, were finishing building the set. The necessary furniture, which was authentic, was already in place. The electrician and his assistant fussed around the floodlights with the brightness of many thousand lumens. Light was one of the most important things in a movie. No wonder so much attention was given to it. Pitch and Co could afford the luxury of setting up an underground set to keep the bright California sun from interfering with the artificial lighting during the indoor filming.

Male and female extras, already made up and dressed in medieval costumes, were peeking around the walls of the set. They all watched the young man standing in the "sun" beam in the middle of the hall with curiosity and barely suppressed smiles. The extras whispered to each other, "It's him."

"Antonio Presto."

"My God, he is so funny! He can't stand still for a moment."

Yes, it was indeed "him" – Antonio Preston, the incomparable comedian who surpassed the former screen idols: Chaplin, Keaton, and Banks. His artistic pseudonym captured his essence very accurately. Presto was never still even for a second. Every part of him moved – his hands, his feet, his torso, his head, and his incomparable nose.

It was difficult to explain why his every gesture inspired such irrepressible laughter. But no one could resist him. Even the famous beauty, Lady Trayn, could not keep from laughing, even though everyone who knew her said she never laughed because she wished to hide her uneven teeth. In the opinion of American movie critics, Lady Trayn's laugh was the greatest victory for the brilliant American comedian.

Presto augmented his natural gift tenfold with his unusual acting. He loved playing tragic heroes. Scripts based on Shakespeare, Schiller, and even Sophocles were written especially for him. Antonio played Othello, Manfred, and Oedipus. This would all have appeared obscene, had it not been for Presto's acting filled with disarming sincerity and deep emotion.

Buster Keaton was comical because of the contradiction between his face, frozen into a tragic mask, and the humorous situations he found himself in. Antonio Presto was comical because of the contradiction between his roles, his surroundings, and even his own feelings and his ridiculous, impossible form and his clownish gestures. Comedy had never risen to such heights, where it almost became one with tragedy. But the audience did not seem to notice.

Only one man, a prominent European writer and original thinker, replied to a journalist's question as to whether he enjoyed Antonio Presto's movies, "Presto is terrifying in his hopeless rebellion." However, the writer was not an American, and he said something that was difficult to interpret. What sort of rebellion and against whom did the writer suggest? The phrase was soon forgotten. Only Antonio Presto kept this foreigner's feedback in his memory, because the writer had truly understood his soul. His was a rebellion of a freak, robbed by nature, to achieve a normal life. His struggle was tragic in its hopelessness.

His right to play tragedies was hard won. During the early years of his career he was forced to perform ridiculous roles, pretend, make faces, receive kicks and hits, and fall down to amuse the audience. His diary included the following entries,

"March 12,

"Read the new script last night. It's outrageous. It's an idiotic script with an idiotic role for me.

"Today, I went to see the director and said, 'Could your script writers come up with anything dumber than this? When will it end?'

"He replied, 'When the audience becomes smarter and stops enjoying such films. They bring in the money, that is all.'

"Money! It's all about money!

"'But you degrade the audience by ruining their taste with this tripe!' I exclaimed.

"'If this is your standpoint, you should quit the movie industry and go teach at an aristocratic school instead. Ours is a commercial and not educational enterprise. You must understand this,' the director objected calmly.

"How could I continue speaking to this man? I left him completely enraged. I felt so angry and helpless, that I purposely over-acted this morning, forced myself, played the ape, and fooled around. There! Take it, if that's what you need! I kept thinking – why won't the director stop all my clowning around? But he didn't. He was pleased! During the break, he walked up to me, clapped me on the shoulder and said, 'I see you have come to your senses. That's more like it. You were better than ever. The movie will be a hit. We'll make a ton!'

"I wanted to strangle this man or howl like a dog.

"But what was I to do? Where am I to go? Abandon acting? Kill myself? I went home and played the violin for three hours – it seemed to calm me down. I kept thinking, trying to find a solution, but didn't come up with anything. It's a wall."

Only when he became world famous, the producers were forced to agree to his "whims" and reluctantly let him play tragedies. They soon came to terms with it when they saw that Presto's tragedies were funnier than comedies.

"Hoffman, Hoffman! Do you think this light is falling at a good angle?" Antonio asked the cameraman.

Hoffman, a fat, mild-mannered man in a checkered suit, carefully looked through the lens of his camera. The light fell onto Presto's face in such a way that the bridge of his nose was insufficiently defined by the shadow.

"Yes, the light is falling too sharply. Lower the soffit and shift the floodlight a little to the left."

"Yes, sir!" a worker replied, as if in the army.

A sharp shadow fell onto the "saddle" of Antonio's nose, making his face even funnier. The light was set for the scene by the window – a tragic confession of love from the hapless suitor, a poor minstrel, played by Presto, before the king's golden-haired daughter. The role of the princess was played by the American film star Gedda Lux.

Antonio Presto directed the movies in which he starred. This time, while he waited for Gedda Lux's arrival, he decided to go over some of the crowd scenes with the extras. One young, inexperienced extra kept walking improperly across the set. Presto groaned and asked her to try again. Once again, it was wrong. Presto's arms went up in the air, resembling a windmill, and he shouted in a very high-pitched childish voice, "It's really not that hard to walk across the floor. Let me show you how it's done."

Presto hopped down from his seat and demonstrated. It was a very clear and accurate demonstration. Everyone understood what he wanted. But at the same time, it was so funny that the extras couldn't help themselves and burst out laughing. Presto started getting angry. When he was angry, he was funnier than ever. The extras' laughter became hysterical. Medieval barons and knights grabbed their stomachs and nearly fell on the floor, ladies-in-waiting laughed so hard they cried and ruined their makeup. The king's wig fell off his head. Presto watched this disaster caused by his unusual gift, then stomped his foot, grabbed his head, ran off the set and hid in the wings. Once he calmed down, he returned to the "castle" looking pale and said, "I shall give directions from behind a partition."

The rehearsal continued. All his remarks were very intelligent and demonstrated his talent and great directorial experience.

"Miss Gedda Lux is here!" an assistant announced.

Presto left him in charge and went to take care of his makeup and costume.

Twenty minutes later he returned, dressed as the minstrel. The costume and makeup could not conceal his ugliness. He was incredibly funny! The extras barely kept from laughing and forced themselves to look away.

"Where is Miss Lux?" Antonio asked impatiently.

His partner was making him wait. This would have been unacceptable for any other actress, but Miss Lux could afford such negligence.

She finally walked in and, as usual, her arrival had a great effect on everyone. This woman's beauty was extraordinary. It was as if nature spent hundreds of years, accumulating tiny bits of all things enchanting, storing them away, picking and choosing among great-grandmothers, only to finally assemble the entire glorious arsenal of beauty and feminine charm in one woman.

Antonio Presto's shoe-like nose moved nervously when he saw Lux. Everyone, from the leading actors down to the last carpenter, was now looking at Gedda. The female extras watched her with an almost religious adoration.

Presto's nose was moving more and more, as if he was sniffing the air.

"Light!" Presto shouted in his high-pitched voice, which sounded even thinner and more shrill from anxiety.

An entire ocean of light filled the set. It was as if Gedda Lux brought it with her. Her stage name suited her as well as "Presto" suited her partner.

Before filming, Presto decided to rehearse the pivotal scene – the confession of the minstrel's love to the king's daughter.

Lux settled into a tall armchair by the window, placed her foot in an embroidered little slipper onto a carved footstool, and picked up her embroidery. A splendid brindled Great Dane lay down at her feet. Presto assumed his place some distance from Lux and, accompanied by a lute, started reciting a poem about the love of a poor singer to a noble lady. The king's daughter did not look at him. She lowered her head and smiled. Perhaps, at that moment, she was thinking of a handsome knight, who defeated all his rivals during the last jousts celebrating her beauty and earned her heavenly smile. But the minstrel interpreted her smile in his own way – after all, he was a poet.

He walked closer to her, singing more and more passionately, then fell to his knees before her and spoke of his laugh.

What an outrage! An unprecedented insult! A terrible crime! The princess frowned, her eyes still on her sewing. Her eyes flashed in anger. She stomped her little foot in the gilded slipper, summoned the servants and ordered the insolent poet taken away. The servants grabbed the minstrel and dragged him off to the dungeon. The minstrel knew that he was facing torture and death but did not regret what he had done. He sent his beloved one last gaze filled with love and devotion. He would be happy to die for her.

The scene went off beautifully. Presto was satisfied.

"We can go ahead and film this," he told Hoffman.

The cameraman was ready. He watched the entire scene through the lens. Presto once again assumed his position.

The camera handle spun. The scene proceeded flawlessly. The minstrel sang, the princess lowered her face and smiled about something. The minstrel walked closer to the princess, fell to his knees and began his impassioned confession of love. Presto was on fire. He not only acted with his gestures and the wealth of his facial expressions, but he whispered the words of passion with such sincerity and power, that Lux forgot the sequence of movements and gestures she has been through dozens of times, lifted her head a little and looked at her partner in surprise from the corner of her eye.

What happened next was not in the script and never anticipated by the director.

Presto, with his short legs, his big head, and his shoe-shaped nose, was speaking about love! This appeared to Gedda Lux to be so absurd, ridiculous, comical, and impossible, that she suddenly burst into irrepressible laughter.

It was the kind of laughter that gripped people like a fit of a terrible illness, and did not let them out of its hands, their bodies shaking with strain, their strength waning, tears running from their eyes. Lux laughed as she had never laughed before. She barely managed to catch her breath, before bursting into another peal of endless silvery laughter. Sewing fell from her hands, and one of her golden braids came undone. The Great Dane jumped to his feet and looked at his mistress in confusion. A dismayed Presto also rose to his feet and gazed at Lux, his eyebrows grimly drawn together.

Laughter is as infectious as yawning. In less than a minute, the entire set was thundering with laughter. Extras, carpenters, electricians, decorators, and makeup artists – everyone was overcome with laughter.

Presto stood there for a few more seconds, completely dumbstruck, then suddenly raised his arms, clenched his fists, and took a step toward Lux, his face horribly twisted. At that moment he was more fearsome than funny.

Lux took one look at him and stopped laughing. The rest of the cast and crew stopped just as suddenly. The orchestra had long since stopped playing since the laughing musicians dropped their bows. Presently, a spooky silence settled over the set.

This sudden silence had a sobering effect on Presto. He slowly lowered his arms, turned, walked up to a large sofa, dragging his feet, and fell onto it face down.

"Forgive me, Presto," Lux broke the silence suddenly. "I acted like a schoolgirl, so much film was wasted because of my stupid laughter."

Presto clenched his teeth. All she could think of was the wasted film!

"There is no need to apologize," Hoffman replied to her. "I purposely did not stop filming and I do not consider it a waste. From my standpoint, this new version of the scene by the window is splendid. Indeed, this laughter, the destructive laughter that leaves no room for hope, laughter of one's beloved in response to a passionate declaration of love – is this not worse than the most terrible torture? Didn't this laugh turn the minstrel's love into equally passionate hatred – if only for a moment? Oh, I know our American public, they will laugh as they have never laughed before. The minstrel's bulging eyes, his open mouth. Don't be angry, Presto, but you were never as spectacular as today. Had I not been accustomed to watching you every day, I couldn't have held on to the camera."

Presto sat up on the sofa.

"Yes, you are right, Hoffman," he said slowly and dully. "It did come out great. Our Americans will keel over from laughter."

Suddenly, something unprecedented happened - Antonio Presto himself burst into a dry, crackling laugh, baring his small, widely spaced teeth. There was something so sinister in his laugh that no one joined him.

KILLING LAUGHTER

After the ill-fated filming, Presto demanded his car and, according to his driver, "drove it to death."

Dissatisfaction, rage against life, indignation with the injustice of nature, wounded ego, and suffering of unrequited love – everything that had been accumulating in his soul for years seemed to have burst free in one terrible eruption. He sought to find comfort in mad speed, as if wishing to run away from himself.

"Keep going! Keep going!" Presto shouted and demanded for the driver to accelerate to full speed. They drove down various roads like criminals chased by the police. They really were being followed. As they zoomed by several farms, they ran over a few ducks and geese walking to a nearby pond, and the enraged farmers ran after them with sticks. Twice the car was followed by a police motorcycle, because it was traveling well above the speed limit and did not stop despite the policemen's demands. However, the motorcycles could not keep up with Presto's car. His was one of the best, most powerful vehicles in the country, custom made for Antonio. He loved speed in all things.

At five in the evening, Presto took pity on his driver and let him stop by a small roadside restaurant and have dinner. Presto himself ate nothing and drank a pitcher of cold water.

Once they were back in the car, they kept driving like mad for the rest of the evening and all night. The driver was falling over with fatigue and finally said that he was falling asleep and could not vouch for the safety of the car and its passenger.

"Keep going!" Presto shouted, but then got out of his seat and took the wheel himself. "You may rest," Presto said to the driver, who collapsed onto the wide back seat and instantly fell asleep.

Presto's thoughts rushed as quickly as the car.

"I have to end this! I have to end this once and for all!" Presto whispered.

When the driver woke up, it was seven in the morning. The car was parked by Gedda Lux's villa.

"Did you sleep well?" Presto asked the driver gently. "I'll just say good morning to Miss Lux, while you wait. Then we'll go home."

Seven o'clock in the morning was early for a visit, but Antonio knew that Gedda Lux rose at six. She led an extremely structured life, according to the recommendations of the best hygienists, in order to preserve the charm of youth and beauty as long as possible – for it was her capital, from which she drew very high interest.

Lux had already taken her bath, had her massage and was going through her morning exercises in a large square room lit through a skylight. Enormous mirrors were set between white marble columns and reflected Gedda from every direction. Dressed in a striped flannel lounge set, her hair cut short and brushed smooth, she looked like a charming boy.

"Antonio? So early?" she said amiably when she saw Presto approaching in the mirror.

She kept stretching, leaning and straightening out as she continued, "Have a seat. We'll have coffee."

She didn't ask what brought him there at such an early hour because she was used to Presto's eccentricities.

Antonio walked up to a large comfortable settee, sat down on the edge, but jumped up immediately and started circling around the room.

"Presto, stop pacing around, just looking at you is making me dizzy," Lux said.

"I must speak to you," Presto said, still walking in circles. "It's about a very serious matter. But I can't talk while you keep rocking back and forth and doing sit ups. Please, do sit down."

Lux looked at Presto, ran over to the sofa and curled up on it, leaving her small shoes on the tiled floor. Presto walked up to her and said, "That's better."

He was clearly making an incredible amount of effort to remain calm, keep his hands and feet from moving and his shoe-like nose from wiggling.

"Gedda Lux! Miss Gedda! I cannot speak… This is difficult… I love you and I want you to be my wife."

His traitorous nose started tipping upward and moving. Gedda lowered her gaze and, holding back the rising wave of laughter, said as seriously and calmly as she could, "Antonio Presto, I do not love you, and you know this. And if there is no mutual love, what is there to unite us? Financial considerations? Common sense speaks against this. Judge for yourself. My net worth and my profits equal your own. I am well off, but I have no wish to reduce my income. Being married to you would decrease my earnings."

Presto's head jerked.

"How so?"

Lux, her eyes still glued to the floor, replied, "It's very simple. You know how the audience idolizes me. There is a kind of cult around my name. For hundreds of thousands, even millions of my viewers, I am the ideal of feminine beauty and purity. But my admirers are demanding toward their deity. Their admiration must be justified. The crowd closely follows every detail of my private life. When I am on screen, even the poorest beggar can look at me and imagine himself as the hero who captured my heart. And that is precisely why I must not belong to anyone. The audience might tolerate it if I married a hero, a man generally acknowledged as the ideal of masculine beauty and virtue. A worthy husband for a goddess must be a god, or at the very least a demigod. If the people discovered I married you, they would be outraged. They would consider this a crime on my part, a mockery of my admirers' best feelings. The crowd would reject me. And the crowd is what brings success."

"And money."

"And money, of course. I wouldn't be surprised if Mister Pitch annulled my contract. I would lose the money, the fame, and my admirers."

"All that for the questionable pleasure of having a husband that looks like me," Presto finished for her. "Enough, Miss Lux. I understand your meaning. You are right." Presto suddenly stomped his foot and screamed in a high-pitched, childish voice, "But what if this freak has a warm, loving heart? What if this freak wishes for his own place in the sun and his own share of happiness?"

This sudden outburst forced Gedda to look at Presto despite her best efforts. His nose was wiggling like a small trunk, the skin on his forehead sometimes gathered into creases and sometimes stretched until it was shiny, his hair was disheveled, his ears were moving, and his arms looked like steam engine pistons working at top speed.

Gedda Lux could no longer take her eyes away from Presto. She started laughing, quietly at first, then louder and louder.

The "scene by the window" between the king's daughter and the minstrel was repeating itself. But there, everything was "make believe", or so Lux thought, while here the minstrel's feelings, his suffering were authentic. Gedda realized the impropriety and offensiveness of her laughter with respect to Antonio, but she could not help herself. Presto seemed to welcome it.

"Laugh! Laugh!" he shouted. "Laugh as you have never laughed before! Laugh! The terrible monster Antonio Presto will speak to you about his love."

And he spoke. He made the most incredible faces. He used his entire vast arsenal of antics and grimaces.

Lux laughed more, deeper, louder. Her laughter was more akin to a fit of hysterics. Gedda convulsed on the sofa in a fit of laughter and looked at Presto pleadingly. There were tears in her eyes. Her voice halting with laughter, she uttered with difficulty, "Stop, I am begging you!"

But Presto was ruthless and relentless. Lux was suffocating. She was powerless and close to fainting. She grasped at her chest, rising spasmodically from laughter, as if she was having a terrible asthma attack.

"People are ruthless to ugliness, may ugliness be ruthless to beauty. My soul is blacker than a scorpion and is meaner than an evil hunchback," Presto screamed.

Gedda Lux realized that he wanted to kill her with laughter. Her eyes widened in terror. Her hands were shaking, she was fading.

Gathering all of her willpower, Gedda reached out to the bell on the side table by the sofa and rang. Her maid entered and found her mistress laughing with a shuddering, suffocating laugh while gazing at Presto. The maid took one look and suddenly grabbed her sides, as if a terrible colic pierced her inside. She sat down on the floor and also burst out laughing. Alas, she was as much in Antonio's power as her mistress.

There was no one left to help Gedda Lux.

YOUR NOSE IS YOUR TREASURE

Hoffman was sitting in a deep leather armchair and smoking his pipe when Presto burst into the room, his eyes swollen from the sleepless night, his face weathered from the wind, and more agitated than usual.

"I waited for you until three in the morning," Hoffman said.

Presto's villa was not far from the Pitch and Co film studio, and Hoffman frequently stayed there for days on end. A well-known cinematographer, Hoffman was Presto's veritable shadow. He watched the actor's every movement, every turn, to capture on film his most original poses and the most successful expressions in the constant movement of his face. Antonio and Hoffman were great friends.

"Where have you been?" Hoffman asked, puffing out a cloud of smoke.

"I was just at Gedda Lux's. I think I killed her with laughter."

"Such is your specialty," Hoffman said, not paying any particular attention to Presto's words.

"Yes, yes… I am cursed for the sins of my fathers."

"Why cursed, Antonio? It's a wonderful gift. Laughter is a precious commodity. This is the way it's always been."

"Yes, but what causes this laughter? It's possible to amuse people with witty thoughts or funny stories. And I amuse them with my ugliness."

"Leonardo Da Vinci said that great deformity was as rare as great beauty. He purposely sought out exceptionally ugly people and drew them in his sketchbook. And you… you are not all that ugly. It's not your appearance that is so comical, but the contrast between your great soul and your miserable body and your marionette gestures. You are well paid for it, and you are incredibly popular."

"Yes, that's exactly right. The great soul! Ah, Hoffman, that is the source of all my trouble. Yes, I am a man of exalted emotions with a body of a cretin. I am deeply unhappy, Hoffman. Money and fame are all well and good while you struggle for them. Love of a woman… I receive hundreds of letters from my 'admirers' from all over the world. But are they guided by love? They are attracted by my wealth and my fame. They are either sentimental old spinsters or miserly souls in search of money, dying to indulge their vanity by being married to someone as famous as I am. And then there is Gedda Lux… Today, I proposed to her for the thirteenth time. She rejected me. But enough. I might as well stop at the devil's dozen.

My greatest source of grief is that I am a dramatic actor. And I am forced to be the clown. You know, Hoffman, that I put my entire soul into my roles, but the crowd only laughs."

Presto walked up to the mirror and shook his fist at his own reflection.

"Stupid mug!"

"You are splendid, Antonio!" Hoffman exclaimed with a chuckle. "This gesture is new. Let me go get the camera."

Presto turned and looked at Hoffman reproachfully.

"Et tu, Brute! Listen, Hoffman, wait, don't go anywhere. Be my friend for once, and not just a cameraman. Tell me, why must things be so unfair? One can change his name, his clothes, his residence, but not his face. You are stuck with it as if cursed."

"Your parents' oversight, perhaps," Hoffman replied. "The next time you are born, demand a photograph at first, and if it doesn't look like a cherub, refuse to be born."

"You are joking, Hoffman, but this is too serious for me. I went from being a miserable little monkey to a millionaire. But with all of my money I can't buy myself five millimeters required to at least make my nose look respectable."

"Why not? Go to Paris, have a surgery. They'll inject some wax under your skin and turn your little slipper nose into a lovely pear. Or better yet, there are now surgical ways to restructure one's nose by moving the actual bones and adjusting the skin. They say there are many such shops in Paris. The signs read 'Nose repairs. Roman and Greek noses are fifty percent more.'"

Antonio shook his head.

"No, it's not what I meant. I know this one girl. She was badly ill as a child with something like diphtheria, which caused the bridge of her nose to fall in. She had a surgery recently. I must say, it helped very little. Her nose is as almost as ugly as ever, and there is now a white scar across the bridge."

"Maybe she had a bad surgeon. Wait, there is something better. I have read in the newspaper recently about a Doctor Zorn living in Sacramento. Supposedly he performs real miracles. Zorn works with some sort of gland – I think it's the thyroid, but I can't remember. And some other gland in the brain that causes not only a person's face to change, but the entire body. He can make a person grow and make his limbs longer. Although, it could be just a scam."

"Which newspaper was it?" Presto asked excitedly.

"Honestly, I can't remember. You can get his address from any newspaper in Sacramento."

"Hoffman, I am going! I am going immediately. Sebastian! Sebastian!"

An old servant entered.

"Sebastian, tell the driver to prepare the car."

"The driver is still asleep, you wore him out yesterday," Sebastian grumbled.

"Yes, that's right, let him sleep. Sebastian call a cab, pack my shirts and suits. I am leaving."

"Don't be crazy, we have work tomorrow," Hoffman said with alarm.

"They can postpone. Tell them I am sick."

"Don't lose your mind, Antonio. After all, if the doctor can really change your appearance, you will no longer be able to finish filming the minstrel's role in *Love and Death*. And you are contractually obligated."

"To hell with the contract!"

"You'll be penalized!"

"To hell with the penalty! Listen, Hoffman, may I rely on you as a friend?"

Hoffman nodded.

"Listen," Presto continued after a thoughtful pause, "I don't know how much time the doctor will need. If things don't work out in Sacramento, I will go to Paris. In any case, I am allowing more time than I might need – I plan to be away for four months. You have long since wanted to visit Hawaii. Go. Get some rest, relax and bring back a beautiful documentary. I know you can't live without your camera. Sebastian will take care of my house. I know I can rely on him. Sebastian! Is my suitcase ready?"

"I am telling you for the last time – give it up," Hoffman said anxiously. "After all, your nose is your treasure."

"Where are you, Sebastian? Have you called the taxi?"

MAGICIAN ZORN

The newspapers did not lie – Doctor Zorn did exist. The first hotel clerk in Sacramento, to whom Presto referred with this question, gave him the address.

"Doctor Zorn! Everyone knows him. He is a true magician!" the man replied.

Presto could not entirely believe it. Perhaps the clerk had been bribed and his answer was nothing more than publicity, but he became more interested in Zorn. Antonio had breakfast and asked for a check, not even waiting to rest from his trip. He had to pay for the entire day, even though he only had one meal.

In a few minutes Presto was traveling across the lush Sacramento Valley. The driver was clearly familiar with the route, having taken many patients to Doctor Zorn in the past.

The car turned off the highway onto a narrower, but equally well-kept, paved road. Drops of machine oil and countless tires polished the pavement to a metallic shine, and it gleamed in the sunlight like a dark river. The scenery changed. The Sacramento River remained behind. Small hills appeared, and groves that were probably planted in this otherwise nearly treeless area – pin oaks, redwoods, pines, cypresses, and olive trees. The clearings were overgrown with cacti, heather, and spurge. There was an occasional orange plantation. Hot breezes carried the scent of pine and wild flowers.

When the driver stopped at a gas station adjacent to a small roadside hotel to refill his tank and have a glass of ice-cold orangeade, Presto stepped out from the car. He was also thirsty.

As usual, he was recognized and surrounded. A smiling hotel owner stood in the doorway, nodding to Antonio as if they were old friends. Women and children looked out of the windows as if they were expecting a movie screen to appear to provide a backdrop for the famous actor's new antics. Antonio winced.

All the attention irritated him more than ever.

While Presto and the driver drank orangeade in a cool, half-lit room, a valet from the hotel quickly refueled the car, deftly wiped the dust off the hood and checked the tires.

"Have you taken passengers to Doctor Zorn before?" Presto asked the driver.

"Tens if not hundreds of times," the driver replied. "But I have never taken them back."

Presto's nose wiggled anxiously. It was so funny that the driver choked and spilled some of his orangeade on the table.

"Pardon me... something in my throat," the driver apologized awkwardly.

But Presto was barely listening to him.

"Do all of Zorn's patients die?" he thought fearfully. "It can't be. Maybe the doctor has his own car fleet. Besides, Zorn's patients are probably wealthy people who have their own cars."

Still, Presto asked the driver, "What are you trying to say?"

"Merely that people who go to see Doctor Zorn don't come back."

Presto looked away – he felt his traitorous nose moving again.

"What do you mean?"

"Well," the driver said, doing his best not to look at Presto and keep from laughing, "the hotel owner in Sacramento can tell you the same thing. People returning from the doctor are completely different from the ones that go to see him, even though they go by the same names. The living skeletons are replaced with stout people, dwarves – with people above average height, freaks – with beauties. They say there was one case when a woman returned as a man with a mustache. The hotel owner recognized her by a large birthmark on the cheek."

"Ah, so that's how it is!" Presto exclaimed with relief.

It was alright then. Apparently, Zorn performed some real-life miracles. Presto would soon be a different man. For the first time he tried to imagine that and suddenly felt uncomfortable. What would happen to the old Presto? After all, this was akin to death and resurrection in a new body.

"Poor, miserable freak! Our life has been tough!" Presto thought to himself. "Still, you managed to get me on my feet, and now I am being ungrateful and sending you to destruction! Should I give up this idea?"

Then Presto remembered Lux and decided to travel ahead to whatever new destiny Doctor Zorn had in store for him.

A sharp turn in the road, and Presto saw a beautiful garden surrounded by an elegant wrought-iron fence. Two marble lions lay by the wide gates. There was also a small gatehouse with Doric columns. The driver beeped. An attendant walked out of the gatehouse, a clean-shaven old man in a white suit. He nodded to the driver, as if they knew each other well, and the car drove through the gates. Beyond was a wide driveway covered with golden-yellow sand. Pin oaks and chestnut trees surrounded beautifully kept flower beds, fountains, ponds encased in stone and reflecting marble gazebos, whose stark whiteness contrasted with the dark greenery of cypress trees, motionless and still in the hot air. On the sides of the driveway, in clearings surrounded by cacti and other evergreen shrubs, were elegant cottages and villas. They drove by a lake – complete with swans and surrounded by weeping willows. Presto looked around curiously and was beginning to doubt despite himself. Did the driver take him to the right place? He saw nothing to resemble a medical establishment. It was more like a summer village for the American wealthy.

But the driver confidently took the car along the lake shore toward a long one-story building with a flat roof and a wide veranda. This was the main office of Doctor Zorn's commercial and medical enterprise. He only dealt with patients who could pay incredible amounts of money for treatment. A talented scientist, an experimental endocrinologist, Zorn was far ahead of his colleagues. He managed to uncover many mysteries of the human body, and discovered ways of influencing the processes that took place within the mysterious glands of inner secretions. As a practical man, he did not publish his discoveries to benefit humankind, but kept them secret, in order to keep the monopoly in his field and make money. Only a handful of people from the lower class were able to take advantage of Zorn's scientific achievements. He wanted to start big right away, but he did not have enough personal capital and had to use loans. To convince his creditors that they were investing in something worthy and reliable, he had to do several demonstrations. Zorn found a few disfigured poor, and even had to pay some of them for the right to experiment with them. Almost before the eyes of the investors, whom he asked for help, Zorn conducted several miraculous transformations. He increased and decreased people's height at will, turned freaks into normal people, and successfully conquered excessive thinness and obesity. The latter had the greatest effect upon the future investors. Obesity was a typical illness among the millionaires leading a sedentary lifestyle and enjoying plentiful meals. Yes, Zorn had indeed stumbled onto a gold mine! Some investors expressed interest in becoming Zorn's business partners. Others suggested that he should set up a manufacturing company for his inventions and take it public. But Zorn was a good enough businessman on his own. Why have partners and stock holders, if he could keep all of the profits from his enterprise to himself? And Zorn opted for high interest loans instead of a public offering. He was right. In a few years, Zorn paid pack what he owed and multiplied his net worth.

His bet was on wealthy patients from the very start. When he set up his sanatorium, he pursued two goals: one, his patients had to have all the conveniences and luxuries they were accustomed to; two, the surroundings, the sunny California climate, and the skill of his groundskeepers were to aid in the treatment. Every patient was offered a separate cottage or a villa – depending on their bank account total – with a complete staff of servants and excellent cooks. The patients had to feel as if they weren't at all in a hospital. Zorn did subject every new patient to a thorough examination, but having established the necessary treatment, he bothered them very little, inviting them to his office no more than once every three days. The treatment consisted of a series of pills, overseen by a specially assigned nurse, as well as intravenous transfusions conducted by his assistants. These procedures only took a few minutes every day. The rest of the time, the patients were free to do as they pleased – read, go boating, ride horses, play tennis, listen to a good on-site symphony orchestra, go dancing or to the movies.

Such was Zorn's establishment when Antonio arrived to check in.

A NEW PATIENT

When Presto entered the office, it caused as much of a sensation as anywhere. People laughed. Curious, smiling faces were peeking around every corner.

A girl in a white coat blushed deeply, suppressing the laughter tickling her throat. She took his check for the amount equivalent to a small fortune and quickly finished all the paperwork.

Presto was offered one of the best villas.

Antonio did not know about the storm that followed after he left the office. Everyone stopped working. All employees left their desks and excitedly discussed the unusual event. Antonio Presto, the incomparable, inimitable comedian, their favorite decided to change his appearance! It was akin to sacrilege. People were no longer laughing. They were surprised, shocked and indignant. America and the rest of the movie-watching world had no idea about the approaching disaster. To deprive millions of viewers of their favorite hero! It was criminal! Presto had no right to do this! He belonged to everyone! The clerk who filled out Presto's paperwork was one of his countless fans. She burst into tears as if she herself signed Presto's death sentence. A young accountant made a speech. He suggested sending telegrams to all the largest newspapers, informing the world about Presto's insane plan, and thus making the entire American public aware of this terrible tragedy, before it was too late. Many supported the accountant's suggestion.

This looked very much like a rebellion. Only one old bookkeeper introduced a dose of common sense. He reminded them of their duty.

"We have no right to make public what takes place in the establishment where we are employed," the bookkeeper said. "This could cause both reputational and material damages to Doctor Zorn. Zorn would be right to fire the undisciplined employees or even sue them for his losses. After all, he would lose a large payment. Besides, Presto is no different from all the other patients seeking Zorn's assistance. He has the right to seek treatment, and no one can stop him."

The bookkeeper's short and calm speech had its effect. The threat of being fired had a particularly strong impact. This wasn't the time to risk one's job. Unemployment frightened everyone. And so the arguments fizzled out and passions cooled. Everyone felt their obligation and their dependence on Zorn and begrudgingly went back to work.

Only the reception clerk kept sighing nervously and whispering while she worked on her papers, "No, no! This must not happen."

SETTLING IN

When Presto entered the villa of white and pink marble, he was greeted by his nurse. She was dressed in a crisp white uniform and a fanciful bonnet pinned to her chestnut hair. With her peaches-and-cream complexion, her smile, and her pleasant young face, she was the embodiment of health. Zorn selected his personnel very carefully, particularly his female personnel. Unattractive, glum and irritable employees were not wanted here. Zorn's patients were surrounded solely by pleasant young faces. This had a positive effect upon the patients' morale. Of course, such faces only emphasized the deformity and various abnormalities of the patients. However, this only made them more willing to pay for Zorn's treatment. This was just another detail in Zorn's well-thought-out system of interconnected medical and commercial goals.

The nurse nodded to him as if he were an old friend – Presto was everyone's friend – and said, "Today you will rest, Mister Presto. Doctor Zorn will see you tomorrow morning. Let me show you the house and how everything works. Oh, Mister Presto, you have exactly the same face right now as in the movie *At the Crossroads*!" and she laughed. It was a good laugh – sincere, youthful, and good-natured. Presto did not find it unpleasant. He even smiled in response, which happened rarely and, as strange as it may seem, made him less funny. He sighed and replied, "Yes, indeed, at the crossroads. What is your name, Miss? Louisa Calhoun? Very well. Show me my new home."

The two-story villa with balconies, verandas and several bathrooms was luxuriously furnished. Not everything about this luxury suited Presto's simple tastes. There were too many carpets, tapestries, bronze, figurines, paintings, colorful upholstery and clashing styles.

"*This suits only the moneybags who know nothing about art,*" Presto thought and remembered his own villa, which he furnished with great care. Here there were pianos and expensive radios, telephones and telegraph transmitters, a library, and a pool table. The servants lived in an adjacent wing. They were expected to appear and vanish like fairy tale genies, following a wizard's magic wand, never bothering the patient when they weren't needed.

"How do you like it?" the nurse asked.

"Excellent! Splendid!" Presto replied absentmindedly. He wanted to be alone. The closer was the moment of "transformation", the more anxious he became. He marveled at his own agitation, because he could not fully understand the reason behind it. It was all decided. There was nothing to be afraid of. It was no different than replacing an old, worn-out suit with a new one. But a troubled voice spoke from his subconscious, "It's not too late to give up this idea."

Once he was alone, Presto walked out onto the second story veranda surrounded by flowering shrubs. He settled down into a wicker armchair to hide behind a blossoming oleander, while he still could see the sandy path beyond the garden fence surrounding the villa.

It was evening. The sun was setting into the invisible ocean somewhere in the distance. The still air was filled with the scent of flowers. Presto lit a cigar and went deep into thought.

The movement on the path distracted him.

An orderly was pushing a three-wheel stroller that was as wide as the back seat of a large car. In it was a shapeless purple mass with barely recognizable outlines of a human figure. The mass jiggled like gelatin or dough ready to spill over. It was a woman with a crimson face, dressed in a purple dress.

An unusual pair followed – a seven-foot tall man as thin as a rail and a female dwarf. The man walked like a crane on his stilt-like legs, while the woman seemed to roll next to him like a little ball. They were engaged in a lively conversation. The giant tipped his head and even leaned down to see the face of his companion. Who knew, perhaps this magician Zorn would adjust their height, make them beautiful and create a new romantic couple.

There was another stroller – a plump man with elephant legs.

"*What a zoo!*" Presto thought, forgetting about his own troubles. Nature's manufacturing clearly had its fair share of defects, and many of them. And these were only those who could pay Zorn tens and hundreds of thousands for treatment. How many poverty-stricken people were forced to live with their disfigurement for the rest of their lives? Presto was lucky to have the opportunity to turn himself into a normal man. It would be stupid not to take advantage of it! Presto's determination to undergo the "transformation" increased.

The telephone rang melodiously on the side table. At the same time, he heard ringing in all the other rooms. He could hear it anywhere in the house and only needed to reach for the nearest receiver. This removed the necessity for a possible added disturbance by the servants.

"Hello!" Antonio said.

"Pardon me, Mister Presto," a male voice said. "This is the doorman. There is a young Miss here who wants to see you."

Presto winced. Must be some nutcase fan who somehow found out about his arrival. Couldn't he get away from them even here? Presto was just about to say that he was tired after his trip and could not see this visitor, when a female voice replaced the male one on the phone, "Mister Presto! I am asking you to see me about a very important matter. It will only take a few minutes of your time."

Her voice was so pleading and, more importantly, anxious, that Presto hesitated. What if it was a patient who wanted to warn him about the dangers of the treatment. After all, Zorn may have had failures too. Presto was also intrigued by the woman's voice. He thought he heard it only recently. A nurse? No, it was someone else. Presto replied, "Very well. A servant will show you in. Tell him I am on the upper western veranda."

Presto was spoiled and didn't consider it necessary to get up and go greet his visitor.

DON'T CHANGE YOUR FACE!

A young woman entered, dressed in a dark blue silk dress. She paused in the doorway, nodded silently, measured the distance between the door and Presto's with her eyes, and approached him without looking at him. Her face was pale and agitated.

"Of course, a nutcase fan," Antonio decided and dryly offered her a seat.

The girl sat down, her eyes still downcast. Presto understood why she did not look at him – she didn't want laughter to interfere with their conversation.

The girl pressed the tips of her fingers to her temples and remained silent, as if gathering her thoughts. Presto waited and puffed out smoke rings.

"Mister Presto!" the girl finally said in a voice that was shaky with anxiety. "We have met before – I checked you in at the office when you arrived."

"What can I do for you?"

"I am violating the terms of my service by coming here and might get fired."

"In that case, you are acting carelessly," Presto said coolly. Even courtesy did not prompt him to encourage or help her – he was afraid that this would open an outlet for uncontrolled emotions that were clearly simmering within her, and bring on passionate declarations of love, admiration, and devotion. He was fed up with such scenes. "What is your name?"

"In this case, my name is of no importance," the girl replied and looked at him for the first time.

Noticing a grimace of displeasure on Presto's face, she blushed, shifted her gaze to the pointy toe of her shoe and exclaimed, "Please, don't think I am a madwoman who came here to smother you with her personal feelings. This is much more serious!" The girl once again pressed tips of her fingers to her temples so intensely that her long red nail sunk into the skin. She suddenly spoke – very quickly, very emotionally, as if delirious, "Antonio! Presto! Don't leave us! Don't change your appearance! Don't deprive us of those happy moments you give us! Please understand, life is difficult, and you are the only one who sheds some light on this hopelessness, helps us forget at least for a short time about the troubles that surround us, gives us respite and new energy, supports us, and places hope into so many hearts that have long since given it up. For the wealthy, you are nothing but a clown who entertains them in their idle boredom. But you are also watched by millions of modest workers such as myself. What will happen to them when you leave the screen? Their lives will become even more hopeless."

Presto was taken aback and even moved. Of course, the woman was unstable. Of course, she was exaggerating. But she raised the question Preston hadn't considered before – the question about the social role of his work. Yes, he would have to think about it. But first, he needed to calm down his visitor.

"Miss," he said gently, "I am very grateful for such high esteem of my work. But you forget one important circumstance. I am a living creature too, and I have a right to have my own demands toward life. Don't you find your demand selfish? 'Keep your shoe-shaped nose for our pleasure.' And why do think you are the only one who is unhappy? Has it occurred to you, that despite all my fame and wealth, I can be as unhappy as the poorest of the poor?"

The girl did not expect such a turn of events. She raised her eyebrows in surprise and asked doubtfully, "You?"

"Yes, me. You said I was nothing but a clown for the rich. Don't you know that some of the greatest comedians suffered from depression and made others laugh when their own souls wept?"

Not wishing to cross the limits of his sincerity or cause any impertinent questions from his visitor, he added, "I have plenty of reasons I don't care to disclose to be unhappy with my fate and to wish to change my appearance."

Whether the visitor was clever, or whether it was her feminine intuition, but she replied in a tone of defeat, "Yes, it happens."

The girl lowered her head, deep in thought. Presto waited.

"I don't know… Perhaps you are right," she finally said. "Such problems are hard to solve. On one side of the scale is your personal life, on the other – the interests of your spectators, your admirers. Not everyone is made to be a hero capable of sacrificing his interests for the sake of others."

This was an open challenge. Presto straightened out and assumed a pose that would have delighted Hoffman. The girl still avoided looking at him and, thus, kept her serious. Antonio was just about to respond to her properly, but the girl anticipated him and exclaimed, "But you will not do this, because you have a generous soul!"

Presto remained silent.

Suddenly the girl fell to her knees before him and said, twisting her hands and almost crying, "Consider this sacrifice! I am begging you! Presto! Antonio! Promise me that you will give up this idea!"

"She is a smart woman but still a nutcase!" Presto thought. He forced the girl to sit back in her chair and said sternly, "Listen to me, Miss. You are trying to break through an open door. You are asking me not to change my appearance. But this is just as illogical as to ask or demand that I keep playing the same role. By changing my appearance, I have no intention of giving up my profession as an actor. Antonio Presto will simply re-appear with his new face and in new roles."

"But our old beloved Presto will cease to exist," the girl said sadly and rose. "I did all I could. Forgive my intrusion and farewell, our dear, unforgettable Presto!"

She left quickly. Presto jumped up from his seat and paced around the veranda nervously, kicking up with his short legs.

"Unforgettable! How about it! It's as if I am already dead! What an unpleasant visit. Nutcase! What right does she have to interfere in my private life?"

Once he had calmed down, Presto started thinking more reasonably. This overly emotional woman shed a new life on his work. Until then, everything was very simple. His unorthodox appearance and talent helped him build a reputation as a world-famous comedian and brought him financial success. He turned laughter into dollars, and that was excellent. True, he had his own creative crisis, of which his admirers knew nothing – in his heart, he was not a comedian, but a tragedian. He was a paradoxical tragedian who inspired laughter! His desire to remove this contradiction, as well as the unrequited love for Lux, brought him to Doctor Zorn. But he never thought that he played an important role in society. More than anything, he felt like an unwilling and ignorant tool in someone's hands. In reality, he took away his viewers – millions of them, in all of America and the rest of the world – from sad reality, distracted them from the gnawing questions and helped them forget their troubles. People didn't just laugh in movie theaters. They took that laughter to their garrets and basements, shared it with each other and improved their lives.

He became even more convinced of this, as he recalled the movies in which he performed. With the exception of classic tragedies – all of them attempts to satisfy the famous actor's whim – all his other scripts either talked about the carefree life of the rich, with Presto playing a supporting role, or about the fate of the poor who miraculously turned into millionaires, allowing every spectator in a threadbare dress and worn shoes to have that dream.

And what about the classic tragedies and dramas performed by Presto! They would have been parodies, obscene mockeries of great works, had it not been for the great and unorthodox power of Antonio's talent, making his Othello and King Lear not only funny, but deeply human and bringing forth laughter through tears from the audience. Still, laughter was Presto's main commodity. This could not be denied. Millions of the unfortunate and the outcasts gathered before the movie screen like cold and hungry travelers before a fireplace, with Presto's laughter to warm them up. Could he take this away from them? Presto remembered when he was a homeless child, and hiding in a movie theater helped him temporarily forget about being cold and hungry, as he laughed at the amusing adventures of the famous comedians of that era. His life would have been more depressing if those moments were taken away from him.

What to do? He couldn't very well give up the transformation, could he?

Presto paced around the veranda anxiously. The sun had long since set, and stars appeared in the dark blue sky, but he took no notice.

"Why can't I continue the same line of work in a new body? One doesn't need to be a freak to act in comedies. Comedies! But what about my dreams about true, exalted tragedy?"

The girl's visit moved him greatly. The step he was about to take turned out to be more serious and complicated than Antonio realized. That night he didn't fall asleep until morning, completely exhausted, having reached no decision. Once asleep, he had nightmares. He dreamed about crowds of people. Men, women, and children reached out to him and shouted, "Don't leave us!" They were led by the girl – "representative of the masses." She embraced him and held him so tightly that he gasped for breath and wheezed.

In the morning, Presto remembered the anxieties of the previous day and night and said, "This is all just nerves!" He took a bath, had breakfast, and went to see Doctor Zorn.

A DIFFICULT CASE

Zorn received Presto in a large study that had nothing in common with an ordinary doctor's office. There were no glass cases with scary medical instruments, no book cases with imposing tomes in various foreign languages to emphasize the erudition of their owner and, therefore, inspire respect, no skulls, and no skeletons. Instead, there was very comfortable leather furniture, a large redwood desk with a heavy sheet of glass resting atop a green cloth covering. On the desk was an inkwell in the shape of a bison, a telephone and two flower vases. More flowers in tall Japanese vases stood around the corners of the room. There were paintings on the walls, mostly sunny landscapes, and two statues – Aphrodite coming out of the sea waves and Apollo, the two ideals of beauty. No price was too high to be rid of one's disfigurement and approach these ideals! The glass wall looked out over a pond and a wide clearing covered with red poppies. This office made the best possible impression on the patients.

Zorn was sitting at his desk, leaning against the high back of his armchair. He was a strong, forty-year old man, with a typical Anglo-Saxon face with ruddy cheeks, aquiline nose and a prominent chin. His short fair hair was smoothly brushed back. Zorn did not wear glasses. His intelligent grey eyes looked both merry and attentive. His thin lips were smiling. A sand-colored suit with a carnation in the lapel was perfectly tailored to his athletic figure. Just as with his office, there was nothing about his appearance to suggest his profession. Everything about this was intelligently and thoroughly thought out.

When Presto entered, Zorn rose and walked up to meet him, like an old friend.

"Hello, hello, Mister Presto!" Zorn exclaimed good-naturedly. "I am very glad to see you. Please, sit down. Right here – you'll be more comfortable."

He led Presto not to the desk but to sit by the window, and settled into another chair facing him. On a small round redwood table were a silver humidor and a lighter.

"Do you prefer cigarettes or cigars?" Zorn moved the humidor with numerous compartments closer to Presto and said, "These are Egyptian cigarettes, Turkish, Cuban cigars *Begueros* and *Regalia Byron* – you won't find them anywhere – and these are from Sumatra, Java, and the Virgin Islands."

Presto thanked the doctor and took a *Begueros* cigar, one of the best Cuban imports. Zorn lit a cigarette.

"When I was informed yesterday that Antonio Presto himself came to stay with us, I didn't believe them right away. Did you really decide to change your appearance?"

Zorn was looking directly at Presto, smiling pleasantly but not laughing, which surprised Presto greatly. Zorn clearly possessed superior self-control.

"Why not?" Presto replied with a question.

Zorn paused, his smile even broader, revealing beautifully kept long white teeth and said, "Can you promise that your admirers won't lynch me for it?"

Presto smiled as well and almost told about his visitor from the night before.

"That is not the only problem," Zorn continued. "I am uncertain whether I have the right to subject you to the transformation."

"The last thing I need is for Zorn to refuse!" Presto thought anxiously and said, "But you perform dozens of them!"

Antonio was agitated and was particularly funny. But Zorn continued to merely smile. He must have possessed an iron will!

"I have only been here a few hours," Antonio added, "and have already seen many fellow patients."

"Yes, but you are an exception. An exception even in my somewhat unusual practice," Zorn objected. "For all of my patients, their physical abnormality is merely an unfortunate side effect. It deprives them of many things and gives nothing back either to them or to society. By receiving the treatment, they lose nothing and win everything. Your situation is very different. Your appearance is intimately connected with your work, with your public appearances."

"Not him too!" Presto thought with vexation and shouted, "I am not a slave to the public!"

"Of course not. You are a free American citizen," Zorn replied. "But presently, I am not talking about you, but about myself. You must agree, that you are an exceptional work of nature, akin to a work of art. Have you seen the gargoyles at Notre Dame in Paris? They are extremely hideous, but there is a kind of beauty about them. What would you say if someone destroyed the gargoyles and replaced them with lovely cherubs? You would have called him a vandal and a barbarian. History would have never forgiven him. He would have disgraced his name. I don't want that to happen to my name. I am afraid that you yourself haven't fully thought out all the possible consequences of your plan. You know that my medical practice is how I make my living. But I am prepared to give up your fee and return it to you to spare myself this enormous responsibility."

"Then you refuse to change my appearance?" Presto said in a defeated voice. At that moment he looked deeply unhappy. Were all of his dreams about a new life, a new body, and happiness to be destroyed?

But it wasn't his miserable appearance that made Zorn feel sorry for him. There was virtually nothing in the world in general that could make him feel sorry. Zorn had no intention of letting go of such a profitable patient. However, it really was a difficult case. Without a doubt, Presto's transformation would cause a world-wide sensation. Of course, there was no danger of Zorn being lynched. But it was likely that newspapers would take him to pieces, and there was no way of knowing whether this would provide a kind of publicity or damage his reputation. Besides, too much publicity was not something Zorn desired. He had enough to work with by attracting clients from the upper class. The general public knew very little about him, and the government did not particularly care, which was just fine with him. Any scandal could attract the unwanted attention of medical organizations, and then who knew how it would end. At best, it could result in losses surpassing Presto's bills, including expenses to sweep the matter under the carpet. That is why he wanted to protect himself in every way possible and even installed a device at his office, recording his entire conversation with Presto. If necessary, Zorn could prove that he did everything possible to talk Presto out of the treatment.

Zorn spread his hands and said, "Your disfigurement is just an illness like any other. As a doctor, I cannot refuse you medical assistance." He said this and the subsequent phrases very loudly and clearly. "This is a very complex contradiction for me, and the best way out would be your own decision. Which is why I can only ask you, with utmost sincerity, to give up your plan. Think it over one more time. Let's wait a day or two. And if you change your decision…"

"My decision is made," Presto exclaimed, "and two days won't change anything."

Zorn sighed and once again spread his hands.

"Very well! The responsibility is now on you," and changing his tone to that of a medical professional, he asked Antonio, "What is troubling you, Mister Presto?"

"Fate."

Zorn nodded compassionately, with an air of understanding, "For us, modern people, fate is nothing but the law of causality. Which is why we no longer grovel before it, but rather twist it into a pretzel. You are my last patient for the moment. My office hours are over. Let us go to the park and have a talk," he added, glancing at his watch.

Presto and Zorn walked down the sandy path toward a remote area of the park.

"So, you are troubled by your fate?" Zorn asked.

"Yes," Presto replied emotionally. "Why is one man born handsome and another one ugly? And this ugliness is like a curse, like Cain's mark. It is unchangeable, unless we count the slow age-related changes from one's infancy to old age."

Zorn shook his head.

"You are wrong. You are very wrong. Not only our face, but our entire body is not something stable or solid. They are variable and flowing like a river. Our body constantly burns, evaporates, and re-builds itself. A second from now you are not the same as before, and after seven years, there won't be a single current molecule left in your body."

"Nevertheless, today I am identical to what I was yesterday," Presto said with a sigh.

Zorn smiled. But this smile was not offensive to Presto. The doctor was smiling at his words, not his gestures.

"Yes, there is the illusion of the constancy of form. But this illusion only exists because our body rebuilds itself following the same pattern as the one that has gone away, burned out as part of our metabolism and vanished. The reason our body re-creates itself that way is because our glands secrete the hormones to guide the reconstruction according to a specific plan."

"Doesn't this imply the constancy of form?"

"Not at all! A statue made of bronze doesn't change until it succumbs to the flow of time. It has a permanent shape. The shape of our body is a different matter. If only one of our glands starts working with the slightest deviation from the pre-defined plan, the shape of our body will begin to change. Here, come look at these patients."

A man of giant height was walking toward them along the path. The proportions of his body were irregular. He had very long arms and legs, combined with a short torso and small head. Despite his enormous height, the giant had a childish face. When he saw Doctor Zorn, he started straightening his jacket, like a little boy afraid of being scolded by an adult.

The giant bowed to the doctor and passed by.

"See how tall he is? Average height of a white male varies between five feet four inches for Italians and five feet nine inches for Norwegians. This giant is six feet eleven inches. He is only seventeen. Until ten years of age he was perfectly normal but then he started growing faster and faster. Why? Because the front lobe of his pituitary gland started developing too fast or, as we say in medicine, this is a result of hyper-function or accelerated activity of the gland. That lady on the right is a dwarf. She is thirty-seven years old, and her height is only three feet two inches. The reason for her lapsed growth is the weakened operation of her thyroid gland."

"Yes, but all these changes happened when they were children."

"Of course, it's more complicated working with adults. But science overcomes all obstacles. Let's go over to that cottage at the foot of the hill. Perhaps we'll be able to see Miss Vede."

A woman sat in a large armchair on the veranda of the cottage.

"Good day, Miss Vede!" Zorn said pleasantly.

The woman nodded to Zorn.

Presto looked at the woman and shuddered. She was a monster with a lengthened face, protruding chin and back of her head, thick nose and lips. She had hideously large hands and feet.

"She is frightening," Presto said quietly when they passed by.

"Yes, she is," the doctor replied. "But believe it or not, this woman was a famous beauty and won a beauty pageant in Chicago only two years ago. Truly, she was incredibly beautiful. I have her photograph from before her illness. I will show it to you."

"What happened to her?"

"For no obvious reason, the bones of her face, primarily her chin, as well as her fingers, toes, ribs and vertebrae started growing. The illness came with overall weakness. The name of this illness is acromegaly, and it depends on the abnormal growth, usually a tumor in the front portion of the pituitary gland. Had it happened in her childhood, she would have become a giantess, but twenty years later this ended up being the result."

"Is she hopeless?"

"Not at all. As soon as we normalized the function of her gland, the shape of her body will change on its own."

"Are you saying her bones will become smaller and she will go back to looking like herself?"

Zorn nodded.

"Doesn't it sound like magic? And here you are talking about the perpetuity of human form. Nothing is permanent. All things change, all things flow."

HORMONES AND GLANDS

Presto slept almost as badly during his second night at the clinic as he did during the first. He couldn't sleep for a long time. Sitting in a large morocco armchair he reviewed the day's astonishing events in his memory. A beautiful woman turned by a terrible illness into a hideous witch, dwarves, and giants, and among all these freaks and monsters was Doctor Zorn, who was like a kind magician preparing to defeat the evil curse and restore them all to looking like normal, healthy people.

Presto dozed off and dreamed that the monstrous woman with the enormous chin rose from her armchair, walked up to him, held out her huge hands and said, "I love you, Antonio. My fiancé left me. But I like you more than him. We are both monsters. We deserve each other. We shall bear freaks unlike any other in the world. They will be so funny that everyone will die laughing. And then our progeny will inhabit the Earth. No one will ever laugh at them, because everyone will be hideously ugly. Ugliness will become the new beauty. And the ugliest of them all will be declared the fairest."

Antonio woke up in cold sweat.

"What a disgusting dream," he thought. He then sat up and grabbed his head. A thought struck him, "In my dream, I ran away from the terrible Miss Vede. But how am I any better? Yes, Gedda Lux was right, a thousand times right by rejecting me. I was unfair and cruel to her the last time. What if Gedda really died from laughter? I left her in a swoon. What if she has a weak heart?"

Antonio jumped out of bed and started pacing the room.

"I should telegraph Hoffman and ask him. Although, Hoffman has probably left. If I really killed her with laughter, there will be an investigation, I will be arrested, possibly charged with murder and executed. And I will die a freak. No! No! If Gedda is dead, there is nothing I can do. No one knows where I went, except Hoffman. First, I must be cured from deformity, and then we'll see. My nerves are completely out of control! I need to calm down."

Antonio forced himself to go back to bed, but still could not fall asleep. "Disfigurement is the worst illness!" he repeated as if delirious. Only when the first morning light touched the tree tops, Antonio dozed off, reciting in his half-sleep the fanciful words that sounded like incantations, "Pituitary… Hormone… Acromegaly… Hyperfunction…"

"No, honestly, I could positively go mad from all this," Presto said when he woke up at eleven in the morning. "I must know exactly what all these hormones and glands are, I must know the entire mechanics of this – then all this fog will scatter and my head will be back in order."

Having bathed, Presto walked up to a large mirror in the bathroom and carefully examined his face. Oh, there was a reason he was a movie actor! He knew every inch of this face – both ugly and funny.

"Big-eared, shoe-nosed freak!" Presto said to his reflection in the mirror. "Soon, you will be no more. You will burn up, flow away, evaporate, and instead… I wish I knew what I will look like after the treatment," Presto said in a different tone.

He got dressed quickly and went to see Doctor Zorn, but the latter was busy with other patients, and Presto went walking around the park instead.

A traveling circus owner would have thought himself in heaven among all these freaks. They would have filled many a company of dwarves and giants. Presto met men and women, fat, barely moving around on their stumpy legs, and as thin as Captain Frackass. He saw men with female busts and bearded women. They were all victims of the random games played by forces unknown to Presto deep within the human organism.

There was a fellow with a huge head and short legs. He was a cretin. He looked at Antonio carefully then burst out into idiotic laughter, "Jim! Jim! Come here, look at this marvel! Antonio Presto hopped off the screen and came to see us! Come, come see a free movie!" he shouted to another patient.

Presto was recognized by everyone who ever saw him on screen. And who hasn't? Cretins and giants attracted by the "live Presto" followed him everywhere. This irritated him. He took a sharp turn to a side path and suddenly emerged by the tennis court. Men and women in white were absorbed in their rounds of tennis. They were completely normal. "These must be the recovering patients," Presto decided.

The disfigured patients stood some distance away. They watched the players with envy.

As Presto found out later, there was a peculiar relationship between the freaks and people who were back to normal. Those still undergoing treatment wanted very much to be in the company with those who had already completed their recovery. This improved their morale and strengthened their hope that they too would soon be equally healthy and normal. But those who were well were reluctant to meet with the freaks and avoided them, because they were reminded of their own recent disfigurement. They became anxious. Some women even looked in their pocket mirrors to make certain that the hideous mask was forever gone from their faces. That is why Zorn's settlement had several societal circles, similar to real life. "Plebs" and "pariahs" – the freaks – gradually transitioned to the "higher" classes as their treatment progressed.

Presto soon was noticed again. He then went to the far end of the park. Beyond a low wall he heard children's voices. That was the children's department.

Once again, the persistent glances of other patients, laughter, and subdued voices followed him, "Presto! Look, it's Presto!"

Alas, here he was one of the lowest pariahs.

Presto went back to his quarters and stayed in until evening. Only after dark, when most patients scattered among their villas, did he finally come out and headed to the doctor's office.

He met Zorn along the way.

"I was coming to see you," Zorn said. "Let's go for a walk. It's good for you. How did you sleep last night?"

"Badly. I think it's the fault of all your glands and hormones. I want to know what sort of animals they are, otherwise, I'll feel as if I am walking around surrounded by evil demons – no better than my distant cave-dwelling ancestors."

"Very well, let us talk about the 'demons'."

"If you don't mind, Doctor, let us follow this path."

Presto pointed at a very secluded path almost no one ever followed.

Zorn nodded and began his explanation.

"You just called the glands in charge of your substance 'exchange demons.' These demons can be both good and bad. How so? I'll explain it. You know, of course, that the human body consists of billions of living cells – tiny pieces of live matter. These small cells, while performing various specific functions, live and work in amazing interaction and agreement between themselves. The more you study the body's functions, the more you are astonished by this harmony of parts, this order and balance that exists among all the cells and systems of an organism. Who sets this order? That is the question that has been of interest to scientists for many years. In the nineteenth century, the scientists assumed that all bits and pieces of an organism were connected by the nervous system, of which the brain was the center, all other cells blindly obeying it. However, it soon turned out that this wasn't exactly true. The brain had a more modest, albeit still very important role. It was the center for transmitting the stimuli from one part of the body to another. This transmission is called 'reflex.' But our reflexes cannot exclusively explain all of the organism's function, and thus the central nervous system is not the main one. There are, essentially, several nervous systems, and the brain is not the primary center for the entire body. It turned out that the organism is controlled in a more complex way. The cells secrete certain chemicals that stimulate the work of glands and muscles. The muscles accumulate sustaining agents and products of substance exchange for the cells, while the glands create a group of chemicals called hormones. These chemicals are not included in the waste produced by the organism and have a very active role in its operation. They are the ones that determine the shape of one's body. The mutual hormonal exchange sets the balance for the entire organism. Billions of cells live in a precisely established interaction. For example, some organs do nothing but produce hormones. Such organs are called the glands of internal secretion. If, for instance, one of these glands works too actively, it begins dominating the rest of the organism, while the role of other factors decreases, and the organism undergoes significant changes – a person becomes abnormally fat or thin, a child grows too fast or stops growing entirely. There are also more substantial changes, leading to physical disfigurement. Thus, the organs of internal secretion, or glands, play the role of controls, and there are quite a few of them: the thyroid gland, the parathyroid, the thymus, the pituitary gland, the adrenal glands, and many others. Speaking of the thyroid gland, where were you born?"

"In the Birkhead Mountains."

"Just as I thought. In the areas located high above sea level, the wind, the rain, and the erosion wash out certain minerals from the soil, necessary for the coordination of the organism and maintenance of certain organs. As the result, the thyroid gland doesn't have enough to work with in these conditions. That is why there are so many people suffering from goiter in your area. After all, goiter is nothing more than the abnormal development of the thyroid gland due to insufficient nutrition. Your illness also originates from the violated balance between the glands. However, this violation is somewhat unusual in your case. You see, people with your ailment usually move slowly, and all of their mental processes are also sluggish. They are listless, slow of thought, phlegmatic, and, frankly, stupid, resembling dim but good-natured animals. Occasionally, a lively mind appears among them. But your mind is not merely lively, it is active, energetic, and creative, combined with the heightened perception and nerve sensitivity. Tell me, do you sometimes have heart palpitations?"

"Yes," Presto replied.

Zorn glanced at his hands.

"You are sensitive, nervous, and impressionable. You are easily excitable, as if two mutually opposing forces are at work in your body. I already have a notion of your character, your temperament, and your mental makeup. You and I will have a lot of work to do. Of course, you want to have a normal height, normal proportions of body and face. In other words, you want to look the way you would have, had the problem with your glands not marked you with its stamp, don't you?"

"Naturally," Presto replied.

"You have never seen your real face. We shall try to discover what it is. I do certain things that other doctors have yet to do. I am called a wizard, a sorcerer. But the same was said about Burbank, the geneticist. What I do is no different from his work. He creates miracles by changing the shape and the entire structure of fruits and vegetables. And I work on changing the shape and contents of a human body. Come, let's go visit my 'museum.' I'll show you some of my trophies. I managed to by-pass my colleagues," Zorn continued, as they headed toward his house. "I managed to create wonderful medicines based on the hormones produced by the glands. With the help of these medicines I manage to change the shape and height of my patients, including adults, in a fairly short period. Look," Zorn said, when they entered the room adjacent to his office, "this is what the power responsible for all these miracles looks like."

He picked up a photo album and showed Presto the pictures within. On the left side were photos of terrible monsters, on the right – those of perfectly normal people, some of whom were very attractive. There was a faint, barely detectable resemblance between the faces on the left and right sides of the album.

"This is before the treatment, and this is after," Zorn said proudly, as he gestured from the left to the right side.

"These are my European trophies. I began my work in France, at Sabatier's clinic," Zorn said. "And here are my first American experiments. Unfortunately, our official healthcare representatives do not look kindly upon my work. The religious circles are complaining too. Although, for the time being, nobody interfered. And here," he pointed at a case with glass doors with white pharmacy jars labeled in Latin, "is something a medieval alchemist would pay a lot for. These are all the different powders. Some of them increase one's height, some decrease."

"Can you really change the height of a grown-up person?"

"Yes, that 'miracle' is within my power. This one here cures extreme obesity, and this one adds weight to extremely thin people. In other words, had I been around five hundred years ago, I could 'enchant' and 'cure' people and make tons of money."

"You would have ended up burning on a stake."

Zorn smiled.

"Most likely. In this day and age, nobody can burn me. But they can still cause me a lot of trouble. Orthodox human thinking lasts centuries."

The doctor ordered Presto to undress, which he did without question. Zorn examined him most thoroughly.

"We must capture the entire sequence of your transformation," Zorn said. "I filmed one patient in the same pose every day. It turned into an astonishing documentary – a transformation from a freak to a demigod right before the audience. But such filming takes a lot of time."

The following day, Presto took the first dose of the powder that was supposed to begin the invisible work within his body.

That day, Presto stood before the mirror for a long time, as if saying good bye to himself.

SACRILEGE

Days followed days, and Presto swallowed one dose after another. He watched himself closely in the mirror, but did not notice any changes. He saw the same shoe-like nose, the same flappy ears, and the same wide head. Presto was losing his patience and was beginning to doubt Doctor Zorn's "magic".

To keep from being the center of attention, he had long since given up his walks in the park and came out for some fresh air only at night. Time went by monotonously and rather boringly. He kept up with the Los Angeles, San Francisco and Hollywood newspapers, wanting to know what was going on in the world.

Several articles attracted Presto's attention, even though they had nothing to do with Lux. In Berkley, California, despite the protests of prim and conservative neighbors, two-year old Ralph Ellison walked around naked for fifteen minutes on sunny days in his back yard. His mother, Lillian Ellison, insisted on it. A doctor recommended sunbathing as a health measure for her son. But the neighbors complained to the police. One emotional husband stated that two-year old Ralph's nudity made his wife feel terribly awkward.

Honorable pastor Noel Gaines from Frankfort, Kentucky stated, "Professors teaching that monkeys were man's ancestors deserve to be hanged."

A university in Arkansas conducted a poll on the topic *Who Is the Greatest Musician In the World*. The results placed Paul Whiteman, the popular jazz conductor, in first place and Beethoven in second. The third place was split between Paderewski and Mister Henry Tovie, the director of the conservatory associated with the university.

Alfred A. Seddon, a Presbyterian pastor of great popularity stated, "Electricity, as a force of nature, has been around as long as human beings – approximately six thousand years. With God's will, why couldn't Adam have a radio in his dwelling for listening to angels' hymns?"

Other newspapers published completely incredible things contributed by the "mind ruler" Robert Ripley. For example, in Boston Ripley discovered one Mister Conners, who established a new record in running up and down a skyscraper staircase. A man named Blaystone used a microscope to write one thousand six hundred and fifteen letters on a grain of rice. A writer in France filled four hundred sheets of paper with punctuation marks and sent them to his publisher for admonishing said author for his careless use of punctuation.

French poet Braytale spent two years writing a love letter to an actress by repeating "I love you" one million times. Miss Cook from London wrote her last will and testament from when she was twenty years old until she was forty. The will amounted to eight volumes, at which point the lady died leaving five thousand dollars. Doctor Littingher in Vienna smiled for thirty days on end.

Such articles interested Presto in that they helped him study the psychology of an average American, his gullibility originating from ignorance, and his tastes. He could use some of this information for his future comedy work.

Finally, Presto found what he was looking for.

Newspapers informed their readers about a terrible illness of Miss Gedda Lux. She had a very strange fit that nearly resulted in death. The doctor, summoned by her maid, found Miss Lux unconscious, blue in the face, and barely alive. The doctor had to work very hard to bring her back to life. Lux's maid also felt poorly, although she recovered from the unfortunate fit before her mistress and found it in her to telephone the doctor. The doctor found no traces of carbon monoxide or any other gas that could cause this condition. Neither Gedda nor her maid could say anything definitive about the incident.

A few days later a reporter from a small tabloid managed to get a few bits of information shedding some light on the events. According to him, Miss Lux's maid told her friend, the driver, that her mistress almost died from laughter when Presto had the audacity to propose to her. "Presto was so hilarious that I myself nearly died laughing," the maid said.

Other newspapers did not print this information, considering it too preposterous. Presto may have proposed and been refused. But to die from laughter was unheard of.

One more day later, the same tabloid printed an article that Antonio Presto definitely had something to do with Miss Lux's strange ailment. Several witnesses confirmed that they saw Presto leaving Lux's villa that ill-fated morning. The doctor was called for Gedda Lux shortly after. In any case, Miss Lux filed no complaint, and the law enforcement representatives could not conduct a formal investigation. Suspicion of Antonio Presto's involvement grew stronger considering his sudden disappearance, possibly due to his fear of responsibility for his actions. According to

Hoffman, his cameraman, Antonio Presto went to Europe for medical treatment. Hoffman himself left for Tahiti almost at the same time.

Later the same newspaper specializing in gossip informed the world that the fact of Presto's sacrilegious actions had been confirmed. Antonio Presto really did have the gall to insult Lux by proposing marriage to her. This news was spread by other papers, and soon Lux's admirers of both genders started flooding editorial offices with thousands of letters, expressing their indignation with Presto as well as condolences to the "insulted and befouled" Lux.

"Sacrilegious actions!" Presto thought resentfully. "If I landed in the hands of Gedda Lux's fans right now, they would have torn me to pieces. Such is the trial by mob! Just as well. No one can tell me now that I have no right to change my appearance!"

Presto was glad that he would soon shed this hideous mask!

He walked up to the mirror and once again carefully examined his face. There were no changes.

"Still, Lux did not want to betray me," Presto thought. "It was the maid. Lux! How will she react to me when I appear before her in my new guise?"

Presto was suddenly overcome with such impatience, that despite the presence of many patients in the park, he rushed to see Doctor Zorn.

"Listen, Doctor! I can't wait any longer. Your medicine has absolutely no effect upon me," Presto said.

"Don't worry," Zorn replied calmly. "My medicine is working. But it doesn't happen as quickly as in the movies. The medicine is impacting your pituitary and thyroid glands. They need to accumulate the necessary amount of hormones. The hormones impact the cells. You see how many transitions it takes? Besides, don't forget that you are not ten years old, and your bones are not as yielding as those of a child. When the glands gather enough strength, so to speak, the process will move much faster."

Presto glanced around and saw a beautiful young woman sitting in an armchair. He had only just realized that he burst into the doctor's office during his office hours without knocking.

"Forgive me," he said awkwardly, referring to the woman.

The patient smiled and said, "The doctor and I have already talked over everything we needed." The woman nodded and danced out of the office.

"Is she new?" Presto asked.

"On the contrary, she is one of the old patients," Zorn replied with a smile.

"But I haven't seen anyone like her among the patients."

"No, you haven't seen anyone like her, but you have seen her. That is the lady we saw in an armchair on the veranda. Miss Vede, remember?"

"The terrible monster?" Presto asked in astonishment.

"The very same."

Presto rushed up to the doctor and started shaking his hand.

"Forgive me, Doctor, for doubting your omnipotence!"

"I have a long way to go before omnipotence, but still, modern medicine can help us accomplish a few things. Go and wait patiently."

THE MIRACLE OF TRANSFORMATION

A few more days passed after that conversation – days that were very much like all the previous ones. But finally, "the miracle of transformation" had begun. It happened one morning when Presto was examining his face.

The mirror did not lie – the bridge of his nose was significantly higher than before. Presto calmed down and felt much more cheerful. There could be no doubt – Doctor Zorn's medicines had woken up the inner forces of his organism and gone to work on rebuilding his body.

Every day brought something new. The bridge of his nose very quickly approached a normal look. The fleshy, shoe-like tip of his nose seemed to "dry up" and shrink, growing noticeably smaller. His ears were also decreasing in size. His entire skull was assuming more a proportionate form. The most amazing thing was that Presto started growing. His fingers, arms and legs grew longer – this was noticeable from the shortening sleeves and pant legs.

One morning the pretty nurse came to see Presto and said with a smile, "You are growing, Mister Presto. Congratulations. Soon, this suit will be too small for you. We have a large warehouse of shoes, underwear and suits of various sizes. Should we send you bigger clothes, or are you going to have them made? We have a staff of seamstresses, tailors and cobblers."

Few of Zorn's patients agreed to wear second-hand clothes! Like most of the others, Presto said he would have his clothes made.

Some patients took the wardrobe with clothes of various sizes with them. Most left these suits behind like the skin of the fairy-tale frog princess, to keep from being reminded of the past. The suits were later sold at second-hand stores by Zorn's agents.

The nurse nodded and left.

A few minutes later, Presto was being measured, while the tailor and the cobbler showed him samples of expensive fabrics and leather and various styles of clothing. They were followed by a hatter. By evening, Presto was dressed in everything brand new, only to repeat this process a few days later.

The inner forces became more energetic with time. Having broken through the established pattern, these forces reconstructed the organism with incredible speed. Antonio had soon lost count of all the new changes and acquisitions. When he pulled out his photograph at the end of the first month of the "metamorphosis" and compared it with his face, he became glad at first, and then frightened – the mirror reflected a complete stranger.

This was no longer the Antonio Presto he knew since childhood. Antonio Presto had lost his old face. Presto felt a chill. It was as if his consciousness moved into another man's body. He tried to move his arms – what came out was new, rather smooth and even elegant, but alien. Physical sensations were new and strange. Every gesture became incredibly easy. His limbs became agile and easier to move. The awkwardness in his movement was gone. Presto's gait, having formerly resembled the flight of a bat, became smooth and light. All this would have been very pleasant, had it not been so new – spookily new.

Changes seemed to take place not only in Presto's body, but also in the surrounding world. A child takes years to grow, slowly and unnoticeably. But Presto was growing quickly, like fairy-tale miracle warriors. As he grew, Antonio felt as if the space around him shrunk. The bed, of which he occupied only a third when he arrived, was getting shorter. Tables and chairs grew lower. He no longer had to engage in contortionism to get onto a chair or into an armchair. He kept moving aside the books and writing tools on the desk to make more room for himself. He could now take his own coat and hat off the hanger by standing in tiptoe. In the past, this was nothing but trouble! Like a child, he constantly had to ask for someone's help or amuse people with his attempts to get something high above on his own, or climb onto something too tall. The world was not made for dwarves.

All these changes were pleasant. But it was the differences in his mind that interested Presto the most.

Antonio spent hours before the mirror. He studied his new body. He admired it and marveled at the miracles of science. Yes, now he believed that a human body was not a set of permanently fixed shapes, that all these shapes were flowing and movable like water. One only had to awaken the inner powers of the organism, the builders of the living tissue – the hormones.

Hormones, pituitary, thyroid – these words no longer seemed like confusing snatches of a mystical spell.

"Still, this is all very strange," he said, looking in the mirror.

The young man looking at him from the mirror was elegant, very slender and straight, fairly tall, with a handsome thin nose.

This new body wore a new suit. Presto looked at his old suit, the little checkered suit with short, almost childish trousers. Suddenly this suit seemed pitiful and touching. It was as if it was left over from a dead son or brother.

"Antonio Presto is dead. There is no more Antonio," Presto said quietly.

He suddenly felt sorry for this little freak, who knew poverty, a lonely childhood, and life on the streets.

Antonio recalled when he left the mountains as a boy in search of a job and headed west. It was difficult to get permanent employment because of his height. In one city he sold newspapers, in another he served as a live billboard, wearing a clown's costume and carrying around a poster "Buy Sunshine Shoe Shine!" Other boys mocked him and frequently beat him up. He had to leave once again. Finally, in one city he was lucky to run into a traveling circus. Once again he had to wear a ridiculous costume, but at least nobody beat him. He stood by the entrance inviting in the public and had a lot of success with the audience. With that circus, Presto visited many towns and cities of America. Somewhere in California, in a town that had its own film studio, the director decided to create a move about a traveling circus. The movie was released while the circus was still in town. Presto saw himself on screen for the first time. His role was a small one – he was still working as a barker at the entrance.

Presto was deeply moved by having seen his own image on screen. Antonio Presto – who was still Tom Johnson then – grew up in his own eyes. If someone decided to put him on the same screen where his favorite heroes used to appear, he had to be worth something. He succumbed to a well-known illness – an irresistible desire to be in films. No one knew exactly what caused this obsession – simple vanity, the desire to get rich quick, or a wish to conquer time and death by capturing at least a few moments of one's own life on film. But, once contracted, this fever was as virulent as it gets.

Antonio went to see the owner of the studio and offered his services as an actor. The man laughed in his face. Antonio refused to give up. He found out about the center of American movie industry, Hollywood, said farewell to the circus and went there. For a long time, producers, directors, and cameramen refused to consider him seriously. However, one intelligent cinematographer thought about it and said to a director, "Why don't we use this cretin to create another Jackie Coogan? At least this one will never grow up."

A few hundred feet of film made no difference. The director agreed to a screen test. Presto was nervous and swung his arms like a windmill. The director exclaimed hopelessly, "He has no idea about acting!" but the cameraman didn't give up.

The movie was unexpectedly successful and surprised both the director and the cameraman. Presto's fate took a sharp turn.

Presto tried to remember his entire life. He wanted to verify whether the new Presto knew everything that the old one had been through. Did the physical transformation violate the consistency of his mind? No, his memory was working fine. The new Presto inherited all of the mental capacity of the old Presto. Still, Presto's psyche underwent significant changes. The new Presto was calmer and more positive. He was more in control of his temper and was less prone to fuss and get upset. This too was very strange. It was as if a thin thread within Presto's mind connected his past identity with his present one – the thread of consciousness. If this thread was broken, the old Presto would be gone forever, and this new young man would be a twenty-seven year old newborn. What if this thread did break? Antonio would forget everything that had happened to him before the treatment. What would he do then? Antonio rubbed his forehead, walked away from the mirror, then glanced back at himself.

"Yes, Antonio Presto lost his face."

PERPETRATOR

The transformation was complete. The mirror no longer reflected a hideous freak but a handsome young man, tall and slender. The most astonishing thing was that in the new Presto, with his flawlessly proportioned forms of a normal person, there was still something evocative of the old Presto, a similarity we might notice in two sculptures that differ in shape but belong to the same sculpture. Doctor Zorn examined his creation with the sense of an artist satisfied with his work.

"Excellent," he said. "I wish you great success. The inner processes of restructuring your body are complete, but do pay attention for the next two weeks. If you notice even the slightest change in your face, immediately come to see me."

Presto shook the doctor's hand in delight.

Antonio left behind nearly all of the money he brought with him – almost a hundred thousand dollars. Presto had just enough for the road. He sent a telegram to Sebastian that he would be returning the following morning.

At the appointed hour, the hired car pulled up before the entrance of Presto's village. The old servant ran down the wide steps descending in a gently sloping half-circle toward the sand-covered driveway, then halted in confusion. Instead of his master he saw an elegant young man, who noticed the servant's reluctance, laughed and said in a pleasant baritone, "Don't you recognize me, old man? It's me, Antonio Presto, but I've been to a doctor and, you see, he changed me, rebuilt me anew. Go get the bags!"

But Sebastian didn't move. He was a devoted servant and even more than that. He treated Presto as a loving nanny would treat a child, and guarded his interests above his own. Sebastian knew the dangers facing wealthy people and their possessions in America, and Presto was a millionaire. Sebastian anxiously read about the tricks used by criminals to take control of wealth that didn't belong to them. Presently, Sebastian had no doubt that he was dealing with one of those swindlers who tried to deceive him and rob Antonio Presto's house.

"You are messing with the wrong man," the old man mumbled suspiciously.

Not only the old experienced Sebastian, but even a junior valet wouldn't have fallen for this trick. The deceit was too obvious. It was impossible for a man to change that much!

"Well, what are you waiting for?" Presto asked impatiently.

"Go back where you came from!" Sebastian said rudely, retreating a few steps up to assume a more convenient position by the door. "The master is not at home, and I won't let anyone in without him. I have my instructions."

"Silly man, I am telling you, I am your master, Antonio Presto."

Presto made an impatient gesture with his hand, which reminded Sebastian of the old Presto. From anxiety and indignation of not being allowed into the house, Presto raised his voice, and his last phrase, "I am your master, Antonio Presto," carried a few notes of Antonio's falsetto.

Sebastian once again looked at the strange young man.

"I'll be damned!" the old man thought. "It's as if he is two people in one."

Perhaps, Presto may have taken advantage of that moment of hesitation and convinced Sebastian had it not been for another witness to this scene. The driver became interested in this conversation. He looked askance at Antonio. Of course, it wasn't Presto. Who didn't know Presto? The driver was clearly on Sebastian's side and gave him a surreptitious wink as if to warn, "Don't let this man into the house. He is dangerous."

Sebastian understood this gesture and walked up another few steps. He was now standing up against the door. Presto was losing his patience. He too started going up the steps, but Sebastian was watching the perpetrator carefully. With speed unusual for his age he slipped behind the door and locked it with a sliding bar, a key, a hook, and a chain. In Presto's absence, Sebastian himself came up with all these complicated locks and had a locksmith install them. Now the old man was completely safe and could withstand a siege from an entire gang of thieves.

"Didn't work, did it, boy?" he said with a triumphant smile from behind the door.

Antonio started knocking but Sebastian refused to unlock the door. Pleas and reasoning resulted in nothing. Sebastian stood as firm as a rock.

"Obstinate, stupid old man," Presto cursed.

Under the driver's mocking gaze, Antonio slowly descended the steps, considering his situation. Perhaps his own driver would be more reasonable. Presto went to the garage, next to which was a small cottage where his driver lived. There was a large lock on the door.

"The scoundrel must have rented out my car," Presto grumbled. He had no choice but to go to a hotel. He told the cab driver to take him to one of the best hotels in the city.

Presto barely had enough money to pay the driver. At least he was wearing an expensive, beautifully tailored suit and had high-end luggage with imposing labels from the best European and American hotels. The doorman respectfully opened the door for him.

"Your name?" a young clerk in large spectacles asked Antonio.

"Antonio Presto, movie actor," Antonio blurted out.

In the past, he did not need to introduce himself. Suppressing a smile, doormen, valets, and maître 'ds used to address him without being told. People knew him better than the President. Now he had to introduce himself. But this was not all. The words "Antonio Presto" had an unexpected effect upon the clerk. He leaned back and gazed at Presto in astonishment. Then he said politely but coldly, "You must be a namesake of the famous Presto?"

This was when Presto allowed himself a weakness. He did not wish to convince the young man of something that contradicted the obvious – the clerk simply wouldn't have believed him, just as Sebastian did not. Why put himself into a ridiculous position of someone trying to steal another man's name?

"Yes, a namesake," Presto replied and rushed to the elevator to go hide in his room.

"What will happen next?" he thought anxiously. "Apparently losing one's face is a very unpleasant thing."

Presto was hungry. Thankfully, he could have breakfast and dinner at the hotel without having to pay every time. Presto telephoned to order breakfast. He noticed that the valet was looking at him oddly. Apparently, the news of an unknown young man who was tactless enough to adopt a famous name had spread through the entire hotel.

After breakfast Presto felt better. Everything would work out in the end, and he would have a good laugh about his adventures.

He could now realize the long-time dream he nurtured the entire time while staying at Zorn's clinic. Presto decided to pay his first visit to Gedda Lux. He would apologize to her and… How would she react to him?

Presto once again critically examined himself in the mirror and discovered that he was truly a handsome man. Now he could perform in real tragedies! His dream would come true. He – Romeo, Gedda – Juliet. Presto struck a pose and held his arms out to the imaginary Juliet. *"Splendid… Irresistible. She won't be able to say no. She cannot refuse me now!"* he thought, changed into a fresh suit and left.

REJECTED AGAIN

Gedda Lux's villa was in the suburbs, not far from Mister Pitch's studio and only half a mile away from Presto's own home. Presto had no money left to hire a taxi.

"I'll have to walk," he thought. He consoled himself by telling himself that walking was good exercise. However, he soon realized than even the most prudent things were only pleasant in moderation. To shorten the distance, he decided to follow a new, recently built road.

It was incredibly hot. The stark white of the not-yet-paved road was hurting his eyes. In addition, cars kept going back and forth, followed by clouds of dust causing Presto to suffocate. He had long since forgotten about the amount of dust and exhaust left behind by automobiles, and how unpleasant they were to a man forced to walk. The drivers seemed to mock the pedestrian by purposely honking their roaring horns and raising so much dust that Presto indignantly clenched his fists.

The familiar route never seemed so long.

When Presto finally made it to Lux's villa, he did not look very presentable. His face and collar were gray with dirt and sweat, his hair was stuck together, his suit and shoes were covered in dust. He looked at himself and hesitated whether he should appear before Gedda like that. But his desire to see her forced him to firmly ring the doorbell. The door opened, and Presto saw the same maid he almost killed with laughter along with her mistress. The girl did not recognize him. He looked at his suit somewhat disdainfully, but then saw his face and smiled. This smiled encourage Presto and gave him hope.

"I would like to see Miss Lux."

Thousands of young men dreaming about fame wished to see Miss Lux in hopes of securing her patronage. Tens of thousands of people of all ages and both genders would have considered it a great happiness to see the "divine" Lux. However, had she received all the visitors, she would have never had time for work.

"Miss Lux is not at home," the maid gave the usual reply.

But Presto was familiar with these tricks.

"She must be at home for me!" he said meaningfully. "I am her old friend, and she will be very glad to see me." The girl chuckled at the word "old". "Yes, yes, don't laugh," Presto continued. "I have known Gedda since she was still a little girl. I came to town for a few days on business and decided to come see her. But my car broke down along the way and…" he pointed at his suit, "I had to walk."

"How should I announce you?" the maid asked pleasantly.

This difficult question again!

"You see," Presto said, "I would like to surprise Miss Lux. Just tell her there is an old friend to see her."

The maid opened the door, let Presto into the large waiting room and went to talk to her mistress, telling Presto to wait. This was half the victory.

"Women are curious," Presto thought. "Gedda will want to see an old friend, especially after the maid describes me. And she probably will."

"Please, sir, Miss Lux asked you to join her in the parlor," the maid said, and Presto anxiously walked toward the familiar room lined with soft carpets and scattered with ottomans, cushions, lion- and bear-skin rugs.

Lux was reclining on a settee, but when Presto entered she rose and looked at him in confusion. Another fraud! The tricks these fans and fortune hunters used!

"What can I do for you?" she asked dryly.

Presto bowed.

"I did not deceive you, Miss. I am indeed your old friend, even though you do not recognize me." His pleasant baritone and sincerity of his voice made a favorable impression.

"Please!" Lux said, pointing at a small armchair.

Presto sat down. Lux settled onto the settee, and a long pause followed. Then Presto started talking, casting meaningful glances at Lux.

"To convince you that I am not lying to you, I can tell you something nobody knows, except you and… one other person. I can repeat everything Antonio Presto said during his last meeting with you, as well as your reply. Verbatim."

"He told you about it?" Lux asked.

Antonio smiled.

"Yes, he did. He was very apologetic about… inconveniencing you by making you laugh so much."

"I almost died."

Presto nodded.

"I know."

"But what does this have to do with you?" Gedda asked. "Did Antonio ask you to apologize for him?"

"Yes, he… bequeathed it to me."

"He died?" Gedda asked fearfully.

Antonio did not answer her question.

"Allow me to remind you how you responded to his offer of marriage."

"My God, I had no idea that my refusal would kill him. He was your friend. Did you come to avenge him?"

"Please, do not jump to conclusions and listen to me. You told Presto that there was an impenetrable obstacle between you. That obstacle was his disfigurement. Isn't that right? Which means, if the obstacle was no longer there, he may have had the chance, does it not?"

"Yes," Gedda replied.

"Well then," Presto said, "the obstacle no longer exists. Antonio Presto didn't die, he changed his appearance. I am Antonio Presto. You can no longer say that I am hideous, can you?"

Presto rose from the armchair and took a few steps, like a fashion model at an upscale clothing store. Lux leaned back. Her eyes were filled with horror. Her mind was working feverishly. Who was this strange man? A madman? A criminal?

"What do you want from me?" Gedda asked, barely in possession of her senses.

"I came for your answer and have already received it," Presto replied. "You said yes."

"But you are not Presto. Please, stop torturing me! What do you want?"

"Calm down, Miss Lux. You are in no danger. I am not a madman or a dangerous criminal. I know, it is difficult for you to believe that the strange young man talking to you really is the Antonio Presto you rejected. But I will try to convince you of this incredible fact."

Presto told Gedda everything that had happened to him after their last meeting, showed her newspaper clippings about Doctor Zorn's "miraculous transformations," and finally pulled out a stack of photos depicting all the stages of evolution his body underwent. These photos were more convincing than anything else. Still, when Gedda looked up from the photos at the handsome young man and imagined the old Antonio Presto, her mind refused to believe that such changes were possible.

She pondered. A silence followed, which Presto did not break. He waited for Gedda's answer is if it were a sentence. Finally, Lux looked at him and said, "Mister... Presto..." Antonio didn't like this beginning. In the past, Gedda never addressed him so formally, calling him "Antonio", like a friend. "Let's assume everything you say is true. The wall of disfigurement no longer stands between us. But..."

"How can there be a 'but'?" Presto asked impatiently.

"I listened to you, now you must listen to me. Remember our conversation when you were still Antonio the freak. I told you that one's privilege was also an obligation. Admiration of the crowds gives much, but also requires much. I am raised above all by the will of the movie audience. And I must not fall out of favor with them. I told you that the spectators would have preferred if I remained an eternal bride. Then any office clerk, any groundskeeper keeping my picture could imagine himself in the role of my "hero". The crowd might forgive me if I marry a true hero."

"A god or a demigod you said."

"Yes, someone who was equally revered by the same audience."

"Isn't Presto a god?" Antonio asked proudly.

"You are no longer Presto. That is the problem. You were a hideous god, but you were incomparable in your ugliness. Now you are as handsome as Narcissus, but the crowd doesn't know you. You have turned into an unknown handsome young man. And obscure beauty is worse than Presto's world-famous deformity. I don't want to, cannot allow for someone to say that the aging Lux – I am two years older than you, and you know that – that the aging Lux bought herself with her millions a young husband, an untalented, unknown, but good-looking young fellow. That is an unattractive role for a man with an ego. And you are spoiled by fame and success."

"Who said I am unknown? Am I not Antonio Presto? Presto had simply put on a new mask. But did he stop being Antonio? Is my talent not the same? In the past, I made people laugh, now I shall astonish them to the core. I was a comedian, a clown, but now I can be a tragedian. Oh, how am I going to act! Believe me, the audience will be struck to the very depth of its soul when they see Presto the tragedian on screen. If I was a demigod, I will become god."

"Will be, will become... Those are nothing but dreams. The path to the movie screen is thorny, difficult, and most often impassable to those who dream about fame."

"Why are you telling me all this? Don't I already know that it's not easy becoming famous? But I... suppose I am an unknown young man.

But I have a great inheritance left to me by Antonio Presto – recognized talent, splendid knowledge of acting technique, and, finally, connections."

"But you don't have the main thing – Antonio Presto's incredibly funny shoe-like nose. The crowd will not recognize you."

"I will make them. Watch out, this is your last excuse. When I come back to you, crowned with glory and adored by the audience…"

"Then we shall continue this conversation. But remember, Presto, I am not giving you any promises and am not obligated to you in any way."

"Are you in love? Do you have a fiancé?" Presto asked.

"I have a heart and free will, Presto. Go get your glory!"

IT'S OUR NOSE, NOT YOURS

The new Antonio Presto had an even harder time getting to see Mister Pitch than he had with Gedda Lux. Mister Pitch's precious time was being guarded by several servants, blind and deaf to all arguments, pleas, and reasons. Having despaired in the power of his verbal assault, Presto decided to physically break through the blockade. He shoved aside one of the valets and quickly walked forward. Fortunately, Antonio knew the layout very well and managed to reach Mister Pitch's office fairly quickly, at which point he kept moving until he was behind the office door.

Presto saw the familiar office, furnished with deep leather armchairs, with a rug on the floor, and photos and portraits of various actors on the walls. In the center of the wall was his own portrait. Antonio Presto was shown life-size as Othello with Desdemona's handkerchief in his hands. Presto has been to this office countless times! Pitch had been invariably courteous with him, offered a good cigar, offered him an armchair, and generally took care of him as if he were an honored guest.

Mister Pitch sat in his usual place, by an open roll-top desk and was talking to his legal advisor, Mister Olcott.

"The contract stipulates a fine of five hundred thousand dollars," Mister Pitch said, paying no attention to Presto. "If Mister Antonio Presto ran away who knows where, before finishing the filming of *Love and Death*, then he, Presto is obligated to pay the fine and other losses. Our accounting department prepared a summary of costs of the unfinished movie as of the day of Presto's disappearance, and how much we will lose by not being able to release the picture. It is a sizeable sum. Prepare to file a lawsuit."

"But who do we charge?" the lawyer asked. "Shouldn't we wait for Presto to return? Perhaps, he is no longer alive. There are all sorts of rumors."

"Just as well. We can designate a representative for the trial and freeze his assets. Don't you understand my purpose in this?"

This conversation was interrupted by the valet, who waited behind the door, but then decided to enter the office without knocking, to beg pardon for his inability to detain an intruder.

"Pardon me, sir," the valet said, "but this gentleman," and the valet pointed at Presto, "entered your office, despite all my…"

Mister Pitch looked at Presto. He had his own rules. He instructed his servants most specifically to not let in any of the "sneaky young people," but when one of them somehow managed to make it into his office, Mister Pitch was courteous and gave no indication that his intrusion was troublesome to him.

Mister Pitch nodded, dismissing the valet, and asked very nicely what the gentleman wanted.

"I can give you some information about Antonio Presto," Antonio said.

"Indeed! Interesting. Tell me, is he alive?"

"Yes and no. This one," Antonio pointed at his own portrait in the gilded frame, "this Presto no longer exists. Antonio Presto is alive, and he is here before you in his new guise. I am Antonio Presto."

Pitch looked at Olcott in puzzlement.

"You don't believe me, and that is understandable. My own mother wouldn't have recognized me, but I will prove to you that I am Antonio Presto."

"Please, do not trouble yourself with proof, I believe you," Mister Pitch replied quickly. "What do you want, uhm… Mister Presto?"

"I overheard a part of your conversation that you would like to sue me for leaving before finishing the work with Love and Death. You don't need to. I will pay the fee and your losses. But we can re-shoot the film. And I will once again play the minstrel. Except the new movie will no longer be a comedy but a tragedy."

"Right, a tragedy…" Pitch repeated vaguely. "You are well informed about our business matters. But… this will not work, young man."

"Then you don't believe that I am Antonio Presto."

"I do, I do, but… but you are a completely different Antonio Presto. We don't need you, no matter who you are. Such patterned Apollos are a dime a dozen, while Antonio Presto was incomparable and unparalleled in his ugliness. He was unique. If you are really a transformed Antonio Presto, which I… do believe, then what right did you have to carry out the transformation? You signed a contract with us for ten years, and a series of separate contracts for your participation in certain films. Not a single king had cost as much to his state, as you cost this studio. Why did we pay you such insane money? For your incomparable nose. We bought it from you for more than its weight in gold. Where is it, this treasure? What did you do to it? A diamond the size of your shoe-shaped nose was a cheap trinket compared to the nose of Mister Presto. You had neither moral nor legal right to deprive us of your nose. It was our nose, not yours. Yes, yes! Antonio Presto's nose belonged to everyone like a miracle of nature. How dare you deprive society of this gift? You see, I am addressing you as Antonio Presto. What have you to say in your defense?"

"I shall find my defense in my actions, not words. Let me perform before the camera, and you shall see that the new Presto is worth more than the old one."

Pitch jumped out of his armchair.

"You are not Presto! Now I can see that you are not Presto. You are a young man dreaming of becoming a movie star. You overheard our conversation about Presto and planned out a risky game. Antonio Presto would have never said what you just did. Antonio Presto knows that talent is a secondary matter. The main thing is publicity. Talented people often die on the street, in obscurity, unappreciated and unrecognized by anyone, while publicity can elevate a mediocre person to the height of fame. Presto was incomparable, splendid, enchanting. But may I burn in hell like a piece of old film, if I couldn't find dozens of him in traveling circus shows."

"You have only just said that Presto and his nose were unique."

"Yes, I did, and I will continue saying that. Because we spent a million dollars advertising that nose before it ever appeared on screen. Any move actor's fame is directly proportionate to the amounts spent on publicity. Antonio Presto knew this very well, no matter how high he valued himself. No need to make tragic gestures. Let's assume that you are the real Antonio Presto, or rather, that you used to be him. Let's assume that you have retained Presto's soul and talent. But the movie camera does not film souls, does it? No matter how brilliant you might be, even if you are three times a genius, the audience does not know you, and that is your problem. Creating a new Presto, Presto the tragedian is too troublesome, expensive, and boring. Enough. I am temporarily halting manufacturing of movie stars and geniuses. It's too expensive. We do not need you, young man. Say hi to our old Antonio Presto if you see him, and tell him that we are impatiently awaiting his return and will greet him back like a son, along with his lovely little slipper of a nose."

"I insist…"

"You shouldn't. I admit that you might be a genius. But the audience will only believe that you are a genius only after I decorate your path with the rainbow of dollar bills, and I have to work hard to get them. I wish you all the best in some other field. Perhaps you will manage to find a job as a clerk or an accountant. It won't give you much, but whose fault is it? You yourself have driven yourself from paradise, if you really used to be Antonio Presto." Pitch rang and ordered the valet to see the young man out.

The game was lost.

"Who was this young man? A madman or a swindler?" the lawyer asked Mister Pitch, after the door closed behind Antonio. "You spoke to him as if you half-believed that he was really Antonio Presto."

"Not half, but almost one hundred percent. The thing is that Gedda Lux called me earlier. She assured me that she saw photographs and various other documents proving without question that Antonio Presto changed his appearance through some sort of treatment. It was only when he asked for a screen test, I admit, I doubted a little that he was Antonio Presto. Idiot! He ruined himself. It's all over for him. He is too spoiled by money and success to find a more modest role in life. Being accustomed to living well, he will soon lose all of his property, liquid and real estate. Which is why I am in such a hurry to file a lawsuit."

"You are as insightful as always!" Olcott complimented his boss.

Mister Pitch lit a new cigar, breathed out a stream of smoke, and when it melted away, said thoughtfully, "Just like fame. When there is no money to buy cigars, the smoke of fame vanishes."

Olcott respectfully listened to this awkward simile as if it was a pearl of wisdom.

EXPLOITING THE PAST FAME

Antonio was disappointed about his failure and extremely thirsty. When he left Pitch, he felt a weakness in his legs. And he still had a long and tiresome walk back to the hotel before him. Antonio followed the beautiful wide main street of the miniature village around the movie studio, past the buildings housing laboratories, workshops, homes, and hotels for the actors and staff.

There was a small restaurant on the right side of the road next to the sprawling movie set warehouse, which was frequented by extras on filming days, when they had to spend many hours waiting. Antonio automatically put his hand into his pocket, hoping to find loose change. But there was nothing there, except a wrinkled handkerchief. Presto sighed and wanted to pass by the restaurant, but the temptation was so great that Antonio slowed down and entered.

Two acting beginners were sitting at one of the marble tables – one with fair, another one with dark hair. The dark-haired actor was recently pulled from the crowd of extras, both literally and figuratively – he was still a part of the crowd, but the director put him in the forefront, so that the viewers could separate his face from the mass of other extras. A short while later he would probably get a small cameo. Then he would be considered a real movie actor. The director who promoted this young man was Antonio himself. What was his name? Smith. One of many millions of Smiths. He would have gone through fire and water for Presto. But, alas! Antonio no longer looked like himself, and Smith would never believe him. The young people were drinking fruit juice. What a torture! Presto paused by their table "accidentally-on purpose".

"Mister Smith, I believe?" Presto asked the dark-haired man, tipping his hat. "You don't remember me, do you? I am Johnson. I was one of the extras in the movie *Love And Death*."

Smith gave him a dry nod. He couldn't very well be expected to remember the names of everyone comprising the faceless crowd.

"Antonio Presto says hi. I saw him just yesterday," Antonio continued.

This news had an amazing effect. The young people perked up. Smith offered him a chair and hailed the waiter.

"Really? Where did you see him? What would you like? A cocktail?"

"Orangeade. Two, three orangeades! It's terribly hot," Presto said. "Yes, I saw him yesterday."

"Does he really remember me?" Smith asked.

"Of course, he said you showed great promise. And if Presto said it... Oh, what a great drink!"

"But where is he? What happened to him?"

"He is undergoing medical treatment. I was visiting my sister and saw him at Doctor Zorn's clinic."

"Presto is ill? Nothing serious, I hope? I have read somewhere that he was being treated somewhere. But what is wrong with him?"

"Presto is changing his line. He is switching from comedy to tragedy. In order to do this, he decided to change his appearance. Zorn is a wizard. He turned Presto into a young man that looks exactly like me."

Smith's mouth fell open in astonishment.

"Madman!" he finally said with great conviction.

"Insane!" his friend agreed.

"But why?" Presto asked.

"Because now he is as worthless as... you and me..."

Having satisfied his thirst and walked back to the city, past his own house and Gedda Lux's white villa.

"I am falling swift and low," he thought, while marching along the highway. "I am living at the expense of my past fame, picking up crumbs in bars, like a vagrant, evoking sympathy by telling others that I know myself. No, this cannot continue. But what can I do? I am so hungry... A man who lost his face..."

As he approached the hotel, Presto straightened out his dusty suit to the best of his ability, in order to avoid attracting attention of the suspicious hotel staff. He quietly slipped into his room, bathed and changed. Fortunately, he had another suit in his suitcase, and a change of underwear.

He ordered dinner, as in the good old days – plentiful, sophisticated, and expensive. Having eaten, Antonio went to bed, asking not to be disturbed, and woke up only at ten o'clock in the evening. Even before he fell asleep, he formed a plan of further actions. He decided not to delay, quickly got dressed, handed his keys to the clerk, and left.

BREAKING AND ENTERING

City lights remained behind. Presto had to walk the distance from the hotel to his own house one more time. But this time, the trip was easier. Cool evening air refreshed Presto, as he swiftly walked along the highway. From time to time, he encountered other passersby – poorly dressed people from the American's vagrant, homeless population.

The handsome villa – his villa! – stood off to the side from the road on a small hill, surrounded by eucalyptus trees. There were so many memories associated with it. At one point he thought that having his own house was the epitome of life's success. He spent a lot of time building it – first, in his dreams, then in reality. He invested so much ingenuity and taste both into the overall layout and into every detail. He did not want any shallow, garish luxury in his home. Everything was to be simple, streamlined, but also elegant. He succeeded. His villa was admired. It was written about. It was imitated.

He invested a lot of creativity into adapting the furnishings to his small height. No one could tell that the furniture was built for children and little people just by looking at it. At the same time, it was not ordinary furniture. Some armchairs and chairs had lower-than-normal seats, others – hidden steps and footstools that slid out with the push of a button.

Yes, Presto had a beautiful villa! His car took a sharp turn at this very spot so many times, to deliver Presto to the front entrance a few minutes later. The driver used his horn to announce the master's arrival from a hundred yards from the house, and Presto was invariably greeted by his faithful valet, the old Sebastian, waiting by the open door. Presently, Presto sighed and headed toward the house, slowly walking uphill.

It was almost eleven o'clock in the evening. There was light in a side window – Sebastian was still up. Antonio carefully followed the garden fence to a group of young cypresses and stretched out on warm sand. Stars shone brightly above him. The air smelled of eucalyptus. From time to time, car headlights flickered in the distance and horns could be heard from the highway.

Midnight... The light was still on. Did Sebastian spend entire nights guarding the house? He was capable of anything.

Cars that looked like luminous beetles passed by less and less frequently. Presto was becoming impatient. He rose and started carefully and slowly climbing over the tall iron fence. He knew that the gates were always locked at night. He was glad that he did not keep any guard dogs. Presto did not like them, because the dogs couldn't stand his abrupt movements and always barked at him. Therefore, despite all of Sebastian's arguments, Presto forbade keeping guard dogs. Presently, he was very happy about it – he could walk up to the house safely. Presto was interested in the window that was still lit. Antonio carefully walked up to it. The curtain was drawn. Was Sebastian asleep or not? Perhaps, the lit-up window was merely a trick to scare away any criminals. Antonio decided to wait another half an hour.

Finally, at one o'clock in the morning, he decided it was time to act.

Presto walked over to the opposite corner of the house and pulled himself up to the window. The frame was closed. He had to press out the glass. But how could he do it without making a noise? Presto tried carefully pressing on the glass to keep it from cracking. But it didn't give in. Should he break it? If the old man was awake, it was bound to attract his attention. Antonio pressed the glass lightly with his shoulder. Suddenly, the glass shattered loudly.

"It's over!" Presto thought, running off to the side. He climbed over the fence, lay down on the ground and watched, expecting Sebastian to come out of the house or open the window. But the house was still silent. Several minutes passed, but there were no signs of life. Presto signed with relief. Sebastian must have been sound asleep. The glass was broken. The main obstacle was removed.

Presto climbed over the fence once again and walked up to the broken window. He started carefully pulling out pieces of glass left in the frame. When there were only a few of them left, Presto rushed and cut his right index finger. He wrapped his handkerchief around it, climbed through the window, and confidently walked through the house.

He felt strange. Antonio was in his own home, where he knew every little detail, but nevertheless, he had to slink around like a thief. After all, he was a thief. He came there to steal money from his own safe. Stepping carefully, he crossed the dining room with the walls and furniture made of carved black oak, a large oval living room with the white grand piano glinting in the darkness, the library with tables, book cases and stacks. He had to be careful to keep from running into one of the stepladders scattered between the stacks. Finally, he reached his study and the safe built into the wall by the desk. 5-6-27-15-9 and 32-24-7-8-12. These were the codes for the two circular locks to open the safe. It was a complicated system, but it worked great. It was just as well that the new Presto inherited the memory of the old Presto, and that memory remained true. Was it not proof that he was still the same Presto or, at the very least, the lawful heir to his money and all his property?

Presto started stuffing his pockets with bank notes. Suddenly, he thought he heard soft footsteps in the next room. Presto froze and held his breath. No, everything was quiet. He must have imagined it. He went back to work. Suddenly, a bright electric light blinded Presto and paralyzed his movements.

"Hands up!"

Four policemen stood in the doorway with their revolvers pointed at Presto. Presto looked at them in dismay. He was unarmed. The study had only one doorway. Should he jump out of the window? But Presto, due to his inexperience, didn't bother opening it. If he tried it, the policemen had plenty of time to catch or shoot him. Resistance was impossible. Presto obediently raised his arms. At that time, someone's mocking laughter sounded from behind the policemen's backs.

"I told you," Presto recognized Sebastian's voice, "that this fellow would come back."

In a few minutes, Presto was handcuffed and seated in a police car. At the police department, Presto underwent preliminary questioning, and the policemen laughed when he called himself Antonio Presto. Antonio was so outraged with their rudeness, that he did not bother proving his rights, but demanded a meeting with the prosecutor the following morning.

"Don't be in such a rush. A meeting with the prosecutor is frequently followed by a meeting with the executor. There are probably a few things in your history that are bound to earn you five minutes in the electric chair," the police sergeant told Presto.

AN UNUSUAL TRIAL

In the morning, Presto had a meeting, not with the prosecutor, but with the county judge, who turned out to be a great bureaucrat. There were reasons for his case going to that particular judge. Presto did not know that Pitch took measures to make certain that the new Presto would not be recognized as the lawful heir to the property of Presto the dwarf. If the new Presto's rights were immediately recognized, then he could represent himself in court, or engage the best attorneys to represent his interests by using money – and all this would have complicated things. Pitch would be much happier with appointing a guardian for the estate. The guardian was suggested by Pitch himself from his own staff, and such a person would undoubtedly defend all of Pitch's demands. In any case, they had to stretch and confuse matters as much as possible, and the judge was doing an admirable job of it. Despite the fact that Presto explained very convincingly that he was, indeed, Antonio Presto who changed his appearance, and that taking his own money was not really a theft, the judge insisted, "Let us assume that your photos are real, and not a cleverly chosen collection of people who look alike; that Doctor Zorn will confirm everything you say, if I satisfy your request and invite him as a witness; that the famous movie actor, who brought me many amusing moments, and you are the same person, even though you don't look anything like him. All this does not change the situation. Ancient Roman lawyers indicated that the word theft – *furtum* – originated from the word *furva* – gloom, darkness, because thefts normally occurred *occulte in tenebris, et plerumque nocte*, which means 'secretly, in the darkness and predominantly at night.' What you did was carried out precisely in that fashion."

"Please," Presto objected. "As far as I know, theft implies taking someone else's property, but this property is mine."

"You have no proof of that. You should have established your identity through legal channels."

"By restoring my former appearance?"

"This would be best. At the very least, you should have presented all your information to the legal offices and proved your identity as that of the vanished Antonio Presto."

"In order to do that, I would have to gather documents, collect testimony and so on. I would like to be released from under arrest until the trial."

"On bail. Five thousand dollars."

"Didn't the police take away a sufficient sum when I was arrested? That was approximately a hundred thousand dollars."

"The ownership of that money is questionable."

"I have nothing else. But listen," Presto pleaded, "what other assurances do you need? Can I run from the trial, considering that conclusion of this case will determine my entire welfare? My estate exceeds a hundred million. Would I really run away from it?"

The judge pondered. He found the argument convincing. Of course, Presto would not run from his millions. And of course Presto was who he said he was. The judge has heard about Zorn and the miracles he performed. Presto was not the first person to have to prove his identity. But that was not the main thing. The most important thing was the capital that would return into Presto's hands. Doing a favor to a millionaire was nothing to be trifled with. Mister Pitch would be displeased. But what was he to do? The judge did everything he could.

There was a reason Pitch's lawyer called his boss insightful. Mister Pitch anticipated this sort of hesitation of the judge's conscience and tried to protect his interests from the other direction.

The judge was prepared to release Presto, but at that moment he received an urgent letter from the prosecutor, demanding to postpone the case of the citizen calling himself Antonio Presto and to not take any actions, as there were circumstances that required the involvement of the prosecutor's office.

The judge read the letter and said, "I can't. There is nothing I can do. Your case will be heard by the prosecutor. But in the meantime, you must go to jail."

He would hear no other arguments. From the police station Presto was transferred to a prison cell.

Presto's was one of the most curious and confusing trials in the American court system history. The trial turned out to be a gold mine for newspaper reporters. Not only the papers, but large reputable magazines were discussing the tangled web of the circumstances.

Did a person have a right to change his appearance?

Was stealing of one's own property truly a theft?

Did Presto really turn into a new person?

Should the new Presto be acknowledged as the heir of the old Presto or should he prove his identity?

Had Presto been married, would his wife have a right to demand a divorce based on the fact that her husband became unrecognizable?

Would these changes lead to new crimes?

Would the criminals obtain a kind of shield to hide them from the law?

What was the view of the church from the standpoint of religion and morality?

Did these transformations threatened the very foundations of American society?

All these questions offered limitless opportunities to dazzle with one's wit and show one's erudition.

The information collected by the prosecutor's office was far from favorable for Presto.

The check-in clerk from the hotel where Presto stayed since his return from Doctor Zorn's clinic testified that Presto himself admitted being a namesake of the movie actor, and not the real Presto. Besides, the civil matters department supplied a note that Mister Pitch requested a freeze on all of Presto's accounts and real estate to secure compensation following the breach of contract prior to the theft. Thus, Presto could be accused of attempting to secure his property from serving as collateral in that lawsuit. Presto's only consolation was that Zorn's testimony as well as that of other patients were in his favor. All of them stated that Presto was not a liar but really Antonio Presto who changed his appearance. However, this was of little help. The prosecutor personally visited Zorn's clinic and was struck by what he saw. Contrary to his rule, he gave an interview to the newspapers and stated his standpoint. Alas, Presto's transformation truly turned out to be a difficult case in Zorn's medical practice.

"The right to private property is the basis of our state," the prosecutor said. "Every kind of property assumes not only the object, but also the subject of that right. In other words, you cannot have property without an owner. Whether it is property belonging to an individual, or to a group, the primary carrier of the right to property is always the physical persona, a human being, a face. What will happen to the society, if the property owner decides to change his physical appearance like gloves? Against whom will we file lawsuits? Whom will we fine? How will we fight against abusive bankruptcies? Most importantly, how will we catch criminals, who will change their faces to look like millionaires, the way they now fake their signatures? How will we tell a real capitalist from a fake one?

It will be terrible chaos. Our businesses will halt. Our country will perish in anarchy. No, in this country, we cannot allow the freedom of changing one's appearance. Perhaps, in one's childhood and for medical reasons, Doctor Zorn's methods could be allowed. But never for grownups. That is why I am submitting to Congress the following proposal – to pass a law immediately prohibiting adult people from changing their appearance under the penalty of losing all their property rights, no matter what methods they use, with the exception of surgical intervention in life-threatening situations. As for our defendant, while normally a law cannot be enacted prior to its official confirmation, I believe it is necessary to invoke its sanctions, because its passing is all but certain. Mister Presto must be stripped of all his property. This will serve as a warning to others."

"Are you planning to keep Presto in jail or do you plan to set him free?" one of the reporters asked.

"As we discovered that Presto is not an impostor, his guilt has been reduced," the prosecutor replied. "He may have been sincerely confused regarding his rights of taking his property from himself. Of course, this does not reduce the gravity of his crime, from my standpoint, but it gives me the ability to release him on bail, until the Congress considers my proposal and passes the new law. Depending on the formulation of this law, Presto will either be acquitted or tried for theft."

A FAREWELL DINNER

Presto was released with no money, no home, and no name.

Antonio Presto returned to the hotel. The manager came to his room and politely reminded him that the room was kept for him the entire time he was gone, because he left his things there, and it was necessary to pay the bill.

"Very well, I shall pay tomorrow morning," Antonio replied, pacing around the room.

The manager bowed, gave Presto a mistrustful look and left.

"Where am I going to get the money?" Antonio said out loud.

He walked over to his suitcase, opened it and started shaking out his suits, hoping to find at least a few bills. There were none. And he desperately needed some cash. Should he telegraph Hoffman and ask him to wire several thousand? There could be difficulties when he tried to collect the money. But Hoffman could send it care of the hotel's manager.

Presto pondered the question and absent-mindedly scanned the newspaper. One article attracted his attention. The theater and cinema section featured the latest news – Miss Gedda Lux was marrying Mister Lorenzo Marr. Lorenzo! The rising star, the handsome Lorenzo, the movie actor who frequently starred in the same movies as Presto. Presto always played the unlucky lover, while Lorenzo – the victor. It happened on screen and, apparently, in life as well. There he was, the demigod, to whom Lux gave her hand and her heart! Was he better looking than the transformed Presto? Antonio glanced at the mirror. Yes, Presto was just as handsome as Lorenzo. But Lorenzo had his own name, while Presto had lost his fame along with his face.

Presto felt he should go see her. Damnation! He didn't even have a decent suit. His best one became rumpled and dirty in prison. Presto picked up a pen and quickly jotted down a telegram for Hoffman, "Send ten thousand dollars care of Mister Grin, hotel *Imperial*, Hollywood. Presto."

Then Presto telephoned the hotel's owner and said, "Mister Grin, I hope you are aware that I am fully capable of paying my bill and find myself in a difficult financial situation purely by accident. My friend Hoffman will help me out tomorrow. He will send ten thousand dollars in your name. Please take whatever you need to cover my bill, and give the remaining sum to me."

The owner happily accepted this deal, and soon Presto's pockets were filled with money – over four thousand dollars after covering his debt, because Hoffman sent only five thousand instead of ten. Presto's credit at the hotel was reopened and the faces of the valets once again became respectful. Antonio bought a new suit, hired a taxi and went to see Gedda Lux.

"Miss Lux," Presto said when he saw Gedda. "I came to offer my congratulations. Have you found your god?"

"Yes, I have," she replied.

"Once again, congratulations, I wish you all the best. I have come to terms with my fate of a man who lost his face. Do you believe that I really am Antonio Presto, your old colleague and friend?"

Lux nodded.

"Well then… I have a big favor to ask you. I would like to have a… farewell dinner and invite all my old friends. This will not obligate them in any way. I simply would like to enjoy their dear company one more time, and then… then your Antonio will assume a more modest place in life." Lux did not like emotional scenes and, seeing Presto so compliant, gladly accepted his offer.

"But this is not all," Presto continued. "I would like you to help me ensure the success of my farewell dinner. Here is the list of guests. You will find the names of Mister Pitch and the lucky Lorenzo Marr, Drayton, Grently and Payne, set designer Buling, light designer Morris and a few other secondary actors. I would like for you to invite them for me. When you receive the guests' verbal agreements, I shall send them all formal invitations. Monday, at eight in the evening, in the round hall of the hotel *Imperial*."

The evening was a glorious success. Everyone on the invitee list showed up. Presto had a chance to convince even the most skeptical people that, while in his new guise, he was still the old Presto, who was not only a great actor, but also a wonderful director. Although, the guests came to appreciate the new Presto's acting skills much later. However, his abilities as the director were fully recognized during the dinner, which was set very tastefully. The hall was lit with delicate rosy light, while moonlight fell through the wide open door to the verandah, creating a lovely contrast. Everything was prepared in advance. The invisible orchestra played beautiful melodies. Several people from the press were invited as well, and they found plenty of material.

Gedda Lux was seated in the place of honor, with her fiancé on her left and Mister Pitch on her right. Mister Pitch liked Presto's idea. As he sipped the subtle wine, Mister Pitch tipped his head toward Gedda Lux and said with a smile, "No matter who he is, this new Presto is starting his new life pretty well. I'd say he shows some promise. And besides..." Pitch took another sip from his glass, "his miraculous transformation and his fantastic trial served as excellent publicity. You can't get such publicity even for half a million dollars. Yes, I think he will make something of himself. If he really possesses the old Presto's talent, he is worth working with."

Lux listened and glanced at Presto with interest, while her fiancé listened to Pitch with suppressed anxiety. Presto could turn out to be a dangerous competitor, both on screen and in life. Lorenzo thought he saw Lux look at Presto not only with curiosity but also with tenderness.

Presto raised a glass of wine, as richly colored and transparent as amber, and made a short speech, "Ladies and gentleman! Did you know that in China there is an expression 'a man who lost his face'? This is said about someone who carried out an unseemly deed. There 'a man who lost his face' is ostracized. Of course, we are talking about China – a strange oriental nation. Here, in our country, the most civilized nation in the world, things are different. Here, our face is closely tied to our wallet. As long as the wallet is fully stuffed, we are in no danger in losing our face, in the Chinese sense of the phrase, no matter what sort of mischief we get into. But woe to those who dare to change their physical face, as I did. They are stripped of everything – money, name, friendship, work, and love. How can it be any different in a country where dollar is king? I do not wish my honored guests to think that I am criticizing the wonderful laws of our fair country. Oh no! I recognize the sensibility of these laws and customs. I yield before them. I made a mistake, a fateful mistake, having changed my face, and am now offering a public apology. It is unlikely that I can restore my prior appearance, even with Doctor Zorn's assistance. But I solemnly swear not to change my face again, and beg the society to forgive my mistake, made due to lack of experience, and accept me back into its embrace, akin to the Biblical father accepting his prodigal son. And you shall see, I will be a worthy son!"

This speech, somewhat strange in the middle, was enjoyed by everyone in the end. There was applause. The reporters took frantic notes.

Antonio had a glass of wine, bowed, and stepped out onto the verandah.

"I say, he is great!" Pitch said in delight. "Even the old Presto showed none of this ability to self-promotion. We positively must make him into a man with a name. Where is he? I want to toast to him."

"Me too!" Gedda Lux chimed in unexpectedly and rose from her seat to join Pitch.

They went to the verandah. Presto wasn't there.

"Presto! Antonio Presto! Where are you?" Mister Pitch shouted, spilling the wine from his glass. "Antonio! My boy!"

"Antonio!" Lux called melodiously.

But Antonio was gone. It was as if he vanished into thin air. The guests walked through the entire garden, which belonged to the hotel and was offered for the exclusive use of the party guests for the evening, but Antonio wasn't there. They returned to the hall. Finally, the guests lost their patience and started leaving one after another, discussing their host's odd behavior.

"Perhaps, this too was for publicity?" Pitch said, while driving home in his car with Marr and Lux. "He overdid it a bit, that mischievous Antonio. Everything is good in moderation." Paying no attention to Lux, Pitch yawned indulgently.

VICTIMS OF "SORCERY"

Days flew by, but there was no word from Antonio Presto – it was as if he died. Mister Pitch waited for the prodigal son to return for some time, but then gave up to the demands of time and work. Lorenzo Marr feared Presto's return not only as a competing actor, but also as a rival for Gedda Lux's hand and heart. After the famous farewell dinner Lux suddenly told her fiancé, the glorious Lorenzo Marr, that he should not rush their marriage. Did the new Presto bewitch her, making her wait for his return? Lux herself was out of sorts. Even Mister Pitch noticed that Lux has changed and became listless, pensive, absentminded, and sometimes irritable. Pitch too did not feel too well lately – he felt ill and short of breath. But he had to work! Mister Pitch decided to film an elaborate new production *Triumph of Love* starring Lorenzo Marr and Gedda Lux. Mister Pitch actively prepared for the filming. The stars, the producers, the cameramen, and the architects met at his office every day.

When Miss Lux arrived, she went directly to the study, walked up to Mister Pitch's desk, held out her hand and said, "Hello, sir. I see you are still gaining weight."

"Yes, and damnably fast," Mister Pitch replied.

He has been adding several pounds every day and presently looked like a fat boar.

"And you appear to be ahead of the fashion?" Pitch asked, looking at Miss Lux's skirt. The skirt was much too short.

Gedda looked at it in confusion.

"I didn't shorten it," she replied. "I don't understand what is happening to my clothes. They seem to grow shorter on their own."

"Or you are growing taller," Pitch said jokingly. "And you, Lorenzo, seem to be losing weight at an alarming speed!"

Lorenzo sighed and helplessly spread his hands. He looked very poorly and was so thin that his suit hung around him like a sack. The handsome Marr even seemed to have grown shorter, his trousers stacking in folds on top of his shoes.

"I have been to the doctor. He recommended a high-protein diet."

"Your cheeks look sunken in. If this continues, you won't be fit for filming. There is not enough makeup to make it better. You will have to take a vacation and get medical help."

Having discussed the business matters and the script some more, they headed to the studio. Cameraman Johnson was setting up his equipment. He asked Lux to stand at the line marked on the floor, looked through the visor and said, "You are out of the frame."

Lux looked at the camera and then at the floor. This couldn't be. She was standing almost in the center of the focus.

"Your hair is outside of the frame. You have grown, Miss Lux."

Other people in the studio laughed.

"I am not joking," Johnson added. "On Friday I filmed you in this very spot, here is the line, and the camera has not been moved. You fit perfectly within the frame, and now you are cut off almost halfway across your forehead."

Lux blanched. She cast a fearful glance at her short skirt. Did she, Gedda Lux, start growing? But this was impossible. She was not a little girl. Nevertheless, not only her skirt, but also the shortened sleeves of her top told her that she was growing out of her clothes like a teenager.

Johnson's experienced eye helped make another discovery. Johnson stated that Lorenzo had not only lost weight, but also became about an inch and a half shorter. This was completely incredible, but Johnson was able to prove that this was, indeed, the case.

Everyone exchanged confused glances. The supporting actors who were at Presto's dinner gathered their courage and also stated that something strange was happening to them. Some of them gained weight as fast as Mister Pitch, some grew thinner, some became taller, some – shorter. All the "victims" started to panic. Lux fainted. Lorenzo whined.

The doctor was summoned urgently, and everyone lined up by rank: first, Pitch – he didn't give up his turn even to Lux – then Gedda, who managed to recover from her swoon, then Lorenzo, and then other actors. The medical consultation was set up in Pitch's study.

The doctor carefully examined all the patients, but found no known illnesses. He shook his head vaguely and spread his hands. All their organs were healthy. Everything seemed to be in order. Only Mister Pitch had the obesity-related degeneration of the heart tissue, which was unavoidable at his weight.

"You must actively fight the obesity. Diet, exercise, walking..."

"I tried it. Nothing works," Pitch replied hopelessly. "What if Presto poisoned me with something at his dinner?" The doctor tried to object. "I am not surprised," Pitch continued. "Notice: the only people who gain or lose weight, or change in height are the ones who were invited to Presto's dinner."

"Such poisons are unfamiliar to modern medicine," the doctor replied.

Mister Pitch was not satisfied with the doctor's advice and called a medical council a few days later. But even that brought him no comfort. Their advice was to go to a resort or check into a special clinic that treated obesity.

Mister Pitch wanted to know how Gedda Lux and Lorenzo were doing and called them. Gedda Lux answered in a voice thick with tears and told him that she continued to grow and could barely alter her clothes fast enough.

"What will happen? Filming is impossible," she said, sobbing. "If this continues, I will soon be fit to be shown at traveling circuses."

"You cannot imagine how much I have changed," Pitch wheezed. "I can no longer fit into the armchair and have to sit on three chairs. My body looks like jelly. I fall asleep during every conversation, and fat is suffocating me."

Mister Pitch didn't even recognize Lorenzo's voice on the phone. Lorenzo answered in such a piercing high-pitched voice, that Pitch had to ask twice who it was. Lorenzo had his own troubles. The worst part was that his face was changing – the bridge of his nose sunk in, the tip of his nose grew wider and tilted up, his ears became bigger, and his mouth stretched out.

"I look like a toad," Lorenzo squeaked. "Presto must have bewitched me."

"I have been saying the same thing. But how could he do this?"

"Maybe Doctor Zorn who treated Presto helped him out."

"Zorn!" Pitch shouted. "Whether or not he helped Presto to poison us, I know that Zorn can help us! He and no other. Why didn't I think of him before? I shall call him immediately. We are all going!"

MOUSETRAP

A strange procession of cars drove up to Doctor Zorn's clinic. An entire line of vehicles brought into Zorn's domain a crowd of unusual freaks, as if an entire traveling circus was on the move. Mister Pitch's swollen, globe-like body barely fit into the back of an enormous automobile. Miss Lux towered over everyone. Lorenzo, however, who had lost all of his splendor, was invisible. He became so short that he could not look over the side of an open top car. Another car brought a terrible monster – a promising young actor who showed symptoms of acromegaly.

New patients were quickly settled into the clinic's cottages.

As usual, Mister Pitch was the first to see Zorn.

Zorn told Mister Pitch a very interesting bit of news. On the eve of the ill-fated dinner someone stole from his lab the jars, in which he kept the chemicals from various glands. Mister Pitch no longer had any doubt that all their troubles were caused by Presto, who clearly wanted to use this unique approach to take revenge upon those who turned away from him.

"Is there hope for improvement?" Mister Pitch asked.

"Absolutely," Zorn replied confidently. "All I need to do is influence one of your cerebral glands, and you will quickly start losing weight."

Zorn was right. In three weeks, Pitch lost a third of his weight, at which point Zorn stated that, "We haven't even gotten to the fat, we have just drained the water."

Generally, Mister Pitch was the least troublesome patient. His ailment was easily treated. Lorenzo's and Gedda Lux's ailments were more complex. Lorenzo became so small that when he stood next to Gedda Lux he could be mistaken for her son.

"Don't worry, there are people taller than you," Zorn said to Gedda Lux. "The tallest height known to science is eight feet four inches. There are rumors that the Russian giant Makhnov was even taller at nine feet three inches."

"I will be happy to simply return to my normal height."

"Very well, we shall try to do just that," Zorn assured her.

Lorenzo Marr caused Zorn the most trouble. He became completely depressed, cried, threw tantrums like a child, begged, demanded, threatened suicide. Zorn spent a lot of time consoling him.

The other patients from the film studio obediently waited their turn. Most of them couldn't afford Zorn's treatment, and they were glad that Pitch decided to pick up the tab, stating that "we'll settle it later." Pitch could not allow for another unfinished movie to be thrown out.

A thinner Mister Pitch tried convincing Lorenzo and Lux to remain the way Presto's "poison" made them.

"You will create no less of a furor than the old Presto." Pitch promised them millions, and Lorenzo started hesitating. But then he looked at Lux and declined this enticing offer.

The treatment continued, and everyone gradually assumed their former appearance. Gedda Lux decreased in height, Lorenzo became noticeably taller, and Pitch was almost back to his normal plumpness. Everyone talked about the approaching departure.

A few days before their check out from the clinic, new patients arrived – the judge, the prosecutor, and the governor. But their appearance! The prosecutor turned into a dwarf like Lorenzo, the judge grew as fat as Mister Pitch, and the governor looked like a Negro. And being black in America was no fun, especially for a governor.

The governor got to become acquainted with all the charming traits of segregation. Outraged by his audacity, the passengers almost threw the governor off the train, when he showed up at the dining car. There were also a few altercations at the train station. In those bitter moments, the governor started having unusual thoughts that American segregation laws were, perhaps, not entirely just and humane, and maybe they should be changed.

He was mortally afraid that he might remain black for the rest of his life. He traveled everywhere with two faithful servants who witnessed his transformation and were willing to testify that the governor was not really black during all the altercations and misunderstandings. Yes, Presto had caused a lot of trouble for the governor, by forcing him to walk in the shoes of a black man. The governor took hot baths for several days, soaped up, rubbed himself with a loofa, but his skin refused to lighten. The doctor he called discovered that the governor's skin was not colored on the surface, but had a dark pigment, like people of African descent.

Having listened to the sad stories of the new patients, Mister Pitch stated that they too must have fallen victim to Presto's revenge.

"But how could he do this?" the governor wondered.

"He may have bribed the servants to add the powders to your drinks," Zorn suggested. "This is all a result of the work of your pituitary gland. It produces a certain substance that has interesting properties. A small quantity of this substance injected into one's blood, causes the expansion of cells containing pigment. Scientists did an experiment a few years ago by injecting this substance into the blood of a pale-skinned frog to cause it to turn dark. The frog became a Negro."

The governor made a face, because he didn't like the comparison. These scientists dared to compare a governor with some pale-skinned frog!

"The pituitary gland can impact the color of human skin too," Zorn continued. "You probably know that pregnant women often start having spots on their faces. The appearance of these spots is associated with the circulation in their blood of the hormone produced by the rear lobe of the pituitary gland, causing this dark coloring."

This was even worse! Now he was being compared to a pregnant woman! To stop these unpleasant scientific explanations, the governor asked, "What about treatment?"

"We must regain control of your pituitary gland."

"Then do it!" the governor exclaimed as passionately as if pituitary gland was his mortal enemy.

"I still don't understand Presto's ultimate goal," the prosecutor squeaked. He was sitting in an armchair and thoughtfully looking at his short legs that could no longer reach the floor. "Was it solely for revenge?"

"What else could it be?" the governor asked.

Everyone paused to think about it.

Mister Pitch, who was the smartest of the group, suggested, "Could it have anything to do with your proposal to Congress, and you public speech condemning the change of appearance by adult individuals?"

The prosecutor stared at Pitch in confusion for some time then clapped himself on the forehead.

"I'll be damned!" he squeaked. "You are right. Presto chased us into a mousetrap I built for him with my own hands! He forced us all to commit the same crime we accused him off – the change of our appearance, our face. What if the Congress supports my proposal? I myself insisted on the preliminary implementation of some of the tenets of the new law."

The black governor groaned. He too realized Presto's clever strike. Their position was hopeless! Despite all of Zorn's skill, they might still look a little different after the treatment. And if their faces were changed, then they too would be impacted by the law. The governor, the prosecutor, the judge, Pitch, Lux, Marr – they would all be stripped of their property and left bankrupt.

"We have only one option," the fat judge croaked. "Either we give up the treatment…"

"Absolutely not!" the governor exclaimed. "To remain black for the rest of my life? Never! Besides, we have already lost our faces, although by accident. I have no desire to subject my fate to the whims of court casuistry!"

"In that case, there is only one thing left," the prosecutor concluded. "We must immediately take back our proposal. Especially considering that many millionaires have already changed their faces. Somehow, I didn't think of this before. Presto will be restored in his rights. We have no choice. He outwitted us."

The meeting ended and Zorn went back to their treatment.

Everyone was well on the way to complete recovery. Miss Lux returned to her normal height and restored her former beauty. Lorenzo grew taller. But he was upset that his nose seemed a little thicker than before. He was afraid that he would not be able to finish the film and that his public would not recognize him. However, this defect soon vanished as well.

All the patients decided to check out on the same day. Zorn approved of this decision. He could verify the results of the treatment by mutual comparison; besides it couldn't hurt for those fully recovered to stay a few more days to ensure the stability of their results.

Finally, this long-awaited day arrived. All of the patients from the group "poisoned by Presto" gathered in a large lecture hall. Despite the fact that Zorn was indirectly guilty of their troubles, the patients sincerely thanked him for the successful treatment. The governor made a particularly emotional speech, being overjoyed at being turned back into a white man.

On the way home, he happily ordered to throw out a black man who had the audacity to board the train car for the whites.

PART TWO

BY THE EMERALD LAKE

Presto was sitting on an empty barrel in the shadow of an old pine tree, smoking a pipe and reading Walt Whitman. *"This is interesting,"* Antonio Presto thought. He pulled out a pen and a notebook, sat down on the grass and using the bottom of the barrel as a desk, started writing, "You must admit, that to a perceptive eye all these cities, swarming with miserable grotesques, cripples, senselessly aping jokers, and freaks, must look like some sort of a boring desert."

"Miserable grotesques, cripples, jokers, and freaks! Now there is some material! This could be better than the ugly old Presto!" Antonio exclaimed. He wanted to keep writing, but a young Saint Bernard called Pip heard his voice and barked pleadingly. He was sitting across from Antonio, impatiently digging with his front paws, turning his head and alternately raising his right and left ears. Presto smiled.

"I don't have anything left. All out!" Antonio said. Every morning he treated Pip to the leftovers from his breakfast.

Pop barked haltingly, jumped up and started bounding around Presto. He was asking for a walk. He was an incredibly smart dog. In the morning after breakfast, Pip liked going to the Emerald Lake. Antonio set up his fishing rods, and Pip fixed his eyes on the float. He squealed and started shaking when the fish started biting. He always got the first catch. Sometimes Presto took the fish to the nearest hot geyser, lowered the net into the boiling water and made a second breakfast. Pip did not approve of this idea – he could not conquer his fear of the bubbling, hissing, steaming geyser and refused to come closer.

Presto looked at the Emerald Lake, the looming blue mountains in the distance, then at the book and his notes, and finally at the park ranger's white cottage. Windows and doors were open. Ellen was still cleaning his room.

"No, Pip, I will not go for a walk with you today. I am going to lie here under the tree and look at the sky," Presto said.

Pip sighed noisily. He knew Presto's habits – if he decided to settle down under the pine tree then it was hopeless. They were not going anywhere and the morning walk was lost.

The last few days before the farewell dinner, so memorable to everyone involved, were very hectic.

Earlier, during the trial, the best American lawyers contacted Presto, offering their help. They could not officially represent Presto in court – he had to issue a power of attorney for that. Presto was in the position of one incapacitated at the time, and the court would not have recognized such a document. Which was why the attorneys offered only unofficial, behind-the-scenes influence upon the officials and judges. The best method of influence was through money or through the lawyers' personal connections. Presto had no money, or, at least, the ability to use it, as his assets were frozen. The most influential lawyers had their own fortunes or could take out loans. They could write off their expenses and create anonymous accounts. For that level of risk they demanded monstrous fees. Antonio hesitated.

A few days prior to the memorable dinner, he was visited by a personal secretary and associate of the famous New York attorney Piers. Piers was once on the Supreme Court, but then retired from this honorable post and traded it for a more profitable one, by becoming a private lawyer. He was considered the greatest scholars of law in the country. Most importantly, he kept all his personal connections with some of the most famous legal experts. He did not need to seek out clients – they came to him on their own. But Piers only accepted the cases involving million-dollar lawsuits and inheritances, some of which he outsourced to his assistants. His was a boldly planned commercial enterprise, and Piers quickly amassed a large fortune. And so the famous attorney sent his representative to Presto, allegedly because he was interested in his unique case. This, however, did not stop Piers from setting the conditions Antonio mentally called highway robbery. Presto's estate would be cut nearly in half. For a few days Presto negotiated with Piers' representative, who offered only minor concessions. Completely exhausted by the attorney's sheer wiliness, Presto was forced to accept all his conditions and sign various promissory notes, including those to cover the bills. What could he do? It was the law of the jungle – one wounded animal was attacked by an entire pack of wolves. At least Piers was slightly more honest than the others – he intended to leave some of the estate to Presto. Besides, the case was in good hands. No other lawyer in the States could do what Piers could. Rumor had it that Piers had never lost a case.

Presto could now occupy himself with another, equally important business, which required complete isolation.

Before the start of his treatment Doctor Zorn had told Presto, "You haven't seen your real face yet, the way it should have been before the illness disfigured you in the early childhood."

Presto got to see his real physical face, but it no longer matched the acting of Presto the freak, the way the dwarf's old little suit no longer fitted the new body. The new face and the new body demanded new content, new goals in life, new trends in his art. Presto became convinced of this after his meetings with Pitch, Gedda Lux and others. The question turned out to be more complex than he expected. He had to find a new artistic identity to go with his new face, a new repertoire, new roles. He had to seriously think about all this. Thinking required focus, and in order to have focus he had to be alone.

"Buddha secluded himself too, when he wished to find himself, first in a mango grove on the bank of the Anoma river, and then in the woods of Uruvela. Where can I find my woods?" Presto thought.

He spent a long time choosing where to go. He considered all the various secluded places of his vast homeland, mountains, forests, and deserts. There were many options. But he did not want to go too far into the wilderness, because he had to follow his case. What if his attorney needed something? Of course, Presto intended to give Piers his address, but only to him and only in the strictest confidence.

Suddenly he remembered Yellowstone National Park. A park with acreage exceeding the territory of Belgium! There had to be plenty of secluded places there! He knew he could find quiet places undisturbed by tourists. He could by-pass hotels and rent a room from some ranger or groundskeeper. Excellent! In the meantime, he could tour this famous park, this wonder of the world. In his constant work and hectic schedule, Presto never made time to visit the park. Now he had a chance to do some sightseeing during his trip – this was very important – and then retire to a mango grove and ponder his fate.

Antonio excitedly prepared for the trip. He bought a lot of books, Yellowstone guides, works about cinematography, literature and philosophy. He had to sort out many things. He carefully defined his route, including changes in transport to cover his tracks. When the guests at his farewell dinner were finishing the last few glasses of wine and looking for their host, Presto was already far away.

SCIENTIST RANGER

As much as Presto prepared himself with books and tourist references, he was amazed when he finally saw Yellowstone Park. It was as if nature used it to collect every fanciful form, every contrast, every color, everything that could astonished and enchant. Mountains, canyons, waterfalls, lakes, and forests followed one another as if in a kaleidoscope. Water from hot springs ejected lime particles that cooled, solidified and formed an entire system of terraces, seemingly carved out of marble. These terraces, some narrow, some wide, were fringed with pendants and the fanciful lace of stalagmites. The pure white terraces were followed by the pale yellow ones, then pink ones, blue ones, green ones, brown ones… Presto became particularly interested in one tall terrace called Devil's Kitchen. It was a dark space filled with subdued humming. Bats circled around like giant black pieces of ash, almost touching Presto and his driver with their wings. Then – a new scene called Golden Gates – a lava formation in golden yellow. Then – the Swan Lake – a wild mountainous area with snowy peaks. He considered stopping there, but the view was much too gloomy and wild. They drove on. They reached the geyser area – Harris Geyser, the hot springs Black Rumbler and One-Minute Man emitting its stream of water every minute, and Old Faithful erupting every twenty minutes. Below were the colorful mud springs – pink, yellow, and white. They exploded with hot water every few minutes, and it fell to the ground in fanciful cascades. Presto decided to get further away from all that noise.

A turquoise spring with uncommonly blue and transparent water was reflected in the mirror-smooth surface of the Prismatic Lake. It was surrounded by a multitude of geysers and hot springs, small mountain lakes, emerald streams with waterfalls. There was the strangely-shaped geyser Beehive, then Sponge, then Lion. Beyond, surrounded by topaz- and ruby-colored rocks lay the Emerald Lake. Presto was enchanted by it. If course, just like everywhere else, there were hotels, gas pumps and car service stations, whimsical drink booths sometimes shaped like an enormous bowler hat (a kind of advertisement for a hat company), sometimes – as the statue of Buddha, sometimes – styled as a Chinese gazebo. The annoying advertisements were everywhere – on the walls of the buildings, on the fences, on the roadside trees, even on the rocks. These billboards selling toothpaste, suspenders, razors, and patented medications disfigured the most beautiful views in the world. But the area further away from the road looked relatively secluded.

Presto noticed a lonely little house, a modest bungalow on the mountain slope in the distance. A narrow, overgrown path led to it, barely wide enough for the car. It must have been a park ranger's home. Exactly what he needed. Presto told the driver to head toward the house. The driver obliged him reluctantly, "It's bad for the car."

But they managed to make it up the slope without any trouble. Only in one spot a geyser right next to the path sprayed the car and its passengers with hot droplets of yellow mud.

It was evening. The sun was already setting behind the mountains. The Emerald Lake took on the shades of sunset and shimmered like mother-of-pearl. Presto sighed in delight from this beauty. Would it distract him? No, it would be alright, one could get used even to beauty.

Presto was lucky. The owner of the house was sitting on a tree stump and smoking a pipe. He wore a cowboy shirt with an open collar, tucked into leather breeches, and tall boots that made it more comfortable to walk through tall thorny brush. He wore no hat. His hair had some gray in it. His face was long, somewhat tired, and bearded. He calmly watched the approaching car.

Presto greeted the owner and stepped out of the car. He explained that he wanted to rent one or two rooms. The hotels were too noisy, and he needed some rest and some time to work on his book. He introduced himself as a journalist and a beginning writer. Smith. Adam Smith.

The old man looked at Presto searchingly. Many tourists who wanted cheap accommodations referred to park rangers, asking to stay with them. Every one of them came up with various reasons why hotels were "inconvenient" for them.

The park's management did not approve of tourists renting from the park rangers. This damaged the profits of the hotel owners. That is why, as tempted as they were to earn a little extra money, the park's employees took in tenants only rarely and introduced them as friends or relatives.

Presto noticed that the ranger hesitated and said quickly, "I will pay you as much as I would for a hotel room, even more."

"But you won't find the same amenities," the ranger objected, clearly ready to give up.

"I am not picky. A chair, a table, a bed, a simple meal – I don't need anything more," Presto said. "I only require peace and quiet, and it appears to be plenty quiet here."

"Yes, unless you count the noise from the geysers. But you get used to it quickly and don't notice it anymore. Well, come in and look."

The owner took Presto into the house. It was not quite as small as it appeared from a distance. There were three bedrooms – one of them fairly large, a kitchen, and a full bathroom. In a small room, the owner showed only briefly Presto noticed a curtained bed, a dressing table with a mirror, and a pair of a small woman's shoes. In his host's room there was a narrow bed, a fairly large desk, and a book case. The walls were decorated with well-made taxidermies of birds and a barometer. Above the desk hung small oval portraits of Darwin and Heckel, much to Presto's surprise.

"This is kind of our living room and formal dining room," the host pointed at the large room, "but we usually dine in the kitchen."

"Do you have a large family?" Presto asked cautiously.

"Just my niece and I," the man replied. "This is the room I can rent to you."

The door and window looked out at the flower bed and pine trees on the hill beyond. Presto liked the room, they signed a contract, brought in his suitcases, and let the driver go.

"As soon as Ellen returns, she will straighten out your room. In the meantime, let's go to the kitchen, I'll make us some tea. You must be thirsty after your trip."

"You are very kind, Mister…"

"Pardon me, I haven't introduced myself. John Barry."

Over tea Barry told Presto how many buffalo, deer, gazelles, and bears were in the park, and what kinds of birds. Barry was friends with many four-legged dwellers of the park. Several bears accepted bread from his hands. He then started telling about trees and unusual plants, and not just the ones that grew in Yellowstone Park. Presto was familiar with some of this from the reference books and travel guides. For instance, much was written about the gigantic height and girth of sequoias. One sequoia stump accommodated a piano and a string quartet, with enough room left for sixteen couples to dance. A small print shop was built on another stump to publish *Giant Tree News*. In 1900 Americans created the largest sheet of wood out of a sequoia tree, intending to send it to the Paris Exhibition.

However, the enormous board remained in America, because there wasn't a single ship that dared to transport it to Europe in one piece.

Such stories were told by all tour guides to American tourists, who were so fond of anything colossal. But Barry was a mere ranger, and Presto was surprised by his knowledge and his articulate, literate way of speaking.

"Do you know the history of sequoia's name?" Barry asked with a smile. "There was an Indian chief by the name of Sequoia. Don't think that it was some sort of a savage hunting for his enemies' scalps with his tomahawk. He was a very intelligent man, an inventor of his tribe's alphabet. The Indians named his tree in his honor. American sequoias were discovered by scientists as recently as the nineteenth century and called "California pines" or "mammoth trees". The latter was probably due to the fact that bare branches of old sequoias resemble mammoth tusks. The first English botanist to study sequoias decided to use them to eternalize the name of the English hero Wellington, and called the tree *Wellingtonia Gigantea*. But the Americans became offended and protested – why was their American tree called after an Englishman, and a general to boot? And so, the American botanists called the tree after their own national hero *Washingtonia Gigantea*. However, it turned out that both names were incorrect, because the new tree was of a new species but not a new genus. Which was why the well-earned name *Gigantea* could stay, but the genus name had to be replaced, because it was already given to another tree of the same genus – *Sequoia Sempervirens* – sequoia the eternal. And so, an Indian chief triumphed over the national heroes of Britain and America. The guides are reluctant to tell this story to American and English tourists to avoid wounding their national pride."

"Mister Barry!" Presto exclaimed, unable to help himself. "You know so much. Why do you work as a ranger, and not a guide, at the very least?"

"Precisely because I know so much," Barry replied with a sad smile. "It's less trouble being a ranger. I should be grateful for what I have."

"But you are an educated man!" Presto said heatedly.

"I am just running my mouth before a stranger." Barry paused and asked, "You are not from one of Gardner's newspapers by any chance, are you?"

"No, no! You can be completely honest with me!" Presto rushed to reassure him.

"I do indeed have a college degree," Barry said. "I am a biologist. I used to be a teacher, but was fired for nontraditional ways of thinking."

Presto remembered the portraits if Darwin and Heckel and was able to guess the nature of nontraditional thinking of this intelligent and highly educated teacher.

This was another walk of life that was never portrayed in Pitch's movies! Screenwriters may have heard of such real-life dramas and conflicts, but they were not interested in them for the very reason that the film studio owners were deathly afraid of such topics.

"In the meantime, wouldn't it make a worthy story? Take the Monkey Trial, for instance!" Presto thought.

The park's management has no idea that I hold a degree from Harvard," Barry continued.

"Harvard! Of course I know about Harvard. It's the oldest university in the States," Presto said. "But I imagine it's not easy living here, especially with your niece."

"What choice do I have? Ellen is an orphan. She is the daughter of my late sister. She couldn't find work in big cities. She tried, but without success. She takes care of the house. Sometimes, she takes some work on the side. She was promised a dishwasher position at one of the hotels here. She is a good girl!" he said lovingly, then glanced at the clock and added with some anxiety, "She is running late for some reason, it's dark."

At the same moment there was loud barking under the window and a voice that sounded almost childish to Presto, "Quiet, Pip! Crazy dog!"

"Here they are!" Barry exclaimed happily.

In a moment, a dog pulling a small cart ran through the open door and halted before the master, barking happily and wagging. The dog was followed by a young woman. Her short, chestnut-colored hair gave her the air of a tomboy. Presto glanced over her with the trained eye of a movie actor. Medium height, flawless build, strong, agile body. The girl wore a simple white blouse with a low-cut V-neck and short sleeves, and a short plaid skirt. Tanned bare legs, sandals. Her near-bronze tan was that of a southerner. Her face was not entirely beautiful – slightly up-tilted nose, full lips with a somewhat childish shape, swift and intelligent glance of her brown eyes. The face had a kind of sweetness that attracted more than beauty. Her every movement showed over-the-top energy and life. She entered, still catching her breath after a swift walk and addressed the dog, "Scoundrel! You almost overturned the cart! I bought some flour, sugar," then she saw Presto and said without any awkwardness, "Hello, Mister. Good evening," as if they were old friends.

Presto smiled and bowed.

This sudden appearance of a cart drawn by a dog accompanied by a girl reminded Presto of a circus number from his past. He suddenly felt happy and light-hearted.

The girl shouted at Pip, "Stand still! I'll get this off you in a minute!" and she started pulling packets and bags from the cart.

"Why don't you introduce yourself to our guest properly?" Barry said, looking gently at the girl.

"Oh, right. I am always in a hurry. Pardon me!" she exclaimed, slightly taken aback. "Just let me get Pip out of his harness. Or else he'll try to cause trouble again."

The girl quickly took off the collar harness. Pip shook his head, flapped his ears, and settled down by the door, wagging his tail.

"This is our tenant. Mister Adam Smith," Barry introduced him. "My niece, Ellen Kay."

"I figured as much," Presto said, shaking her small hand. He felt that Ellen's palms were callused.

"The poor girl has to do a lot of manual work," Presto thought compassionately.

As if to confirm this, Barry said to the girl, "Ellen, once you put away the groceries, wash the floor in the living room, then make the bed in Mister Smith's room, and put in a wash basin."

"Please, don't trouble yourself!" Presto exclaimed. "Just give me the sheets, and I can make my own bed, and the rest can wait until tomorrow. It's late, and Miss Kay must be tired."

"Tired?" the girl repeated with surprise and even some offense. She started moving the groceries from the cart to the cabinet with such speed that Presto could barely follow her with his eyes.

"This girl certainly has some energy!" he thought, following her movements despite himself. The pace was a little fast for filming, but there was so much natural grace in these simple movements! What movie actors achieved with great difficulty, after endless drilling by directors and hundreds of feet of ruined film, she did naturally, and she didn't even suspect it, pondering about the beauty of her movements no more than a playful kitten.

In less than three minutes, all the groceries and the cart were put away.

"One more thing!" the girl said, as if continuing an argument, "Call me Ellen. I am not grownup enough to be Miss Kay!"

The girl gave him an almost angry glance and went to the living room. In a minute she was already hard at work there, moving furniture and humming a tune.

"You have a fantastic housekeeper," Presto said.

"Yes. I told you she was a great girl," Barry said, clearly proud of his niece. "She is very capable too! She could achieve much." Barry's face darkened.

Presto understood the ranger's thoughts and said, trying to console him, "There is still plenty of time, she is barely more than a child."

"She is not as young as she looks. She is almost eighteen. And I failed to give her even a high school education."

They paused, each with his thoughts.

EUREKA

And so, Presto moved into John Barry's house.

Every morning Antonio took time to read and think. He read books on the history of American cinema, pondered the faces and masks of famous actors, as they searched for their identity, their new original persona. In the evenings, he talked with the educated ranger and his niece.

Ellen stayed away from him at first. But Presto brought many new publications with him, and Ellen was extremely interested in them. In a few days she felt brave enough to argue with Presto about the novels she'd read, surprising him with her astute and original opinions. It turned out that she was very familiar with European classics and American literature. Once, she read Desdemona's monologue to him, and then acted the scene of Ophelia's madness. Presto was astounded. Ellen unquestionably had a dramatic talent. What if he could turn her into an actress, a partner in serious tragedies?

But the next morning Ophelia went back to being a maid, a dishwasher, and a cook.

As soon as Presto woke up, Ellen showed up with buckets, rags, and mops, kicked out Presto and Pip into the garden and started cleaning the room.

While he lay under the pine tree on the hill, Presto secretly watched her. Of course, it wasn't very nice. But he justified himself by reasoning that observing other people was his professional duty and all his observations could come in useful in his work.

Ellen gathered her short striped skirt between her knees, leaned over and washed the floor. When she swept the cobwebs and dust off the ceiling, she stretched up and leaned back a little. Her pose changed every second. Presto watched Ellen and thought, *"If only Hoffman could see her! He would have been delighted by this turn. I have never suspected how much grace and beauty there was in simple working movements. Amazing! Our famous actresses, our movie stars have to use so many tricks, artificial poses, turns, and angles to show their figures to the best advantage, to emphasize a beautiful line of the waist, the hip, the back, or a graceful leg, to hide they are natural drawbacks! All this invariably restricts the freedom of their movements, and turns them into beautiful automatons or mannequins. The director has to work hard to make their movements seem natural and simple!"*

Presto remembered when one director made an actress do a simple movement with her foot dozens of times, and used up hundreds of feet of film before he got what he wanted. All of Ellen's movements, on the other hand, were efficient and effective, not a single gesture was lost.

"No, there is no need to make her into Ophelia or Desdemona. She would have to be trained, forced into unnatural gesturing and into thinking about her every move. Ellen would fall prey to the same thing as that centipede in Oscar Wilde's tale, who ran about until it was asked to explain precisely how it moved its legs – which moved first, and which moved second. The centipede got to thinking about it and couldn't take a single step. Ellen must remain herself. Which means we need new story lines and new scripts."

Presto's thoughts were interrupted by Ellen. She leaned out of the window and shouted louder than necessary, "Mister Smith! The cinema next to Rossetti's hotel is playing a film with Antonio Presto this evening."

"Are you going?" Presto said.

"Absolutely!" the girl replied. "There have been no new movies with him lately. They say he disappeared or something bad happened to him. That would be terrible!"

"Do you love Antonio Presto?"

"Who doesn't?" Ellen replied.

Presto enjoyed hearing this, but the girl's following sentence was somewhat upsetting.

"Everyone loves a good laugh, and he is so funny. I absolutely adore him."

"Would you marry him if he offered?"

Ellen was surprised by the question.

"Marry him?" she exclaimed with revulsion and some indignation for being asked such a question. "Never!"

"Why?" Antonio asked, already knowing what the answer would be. But it turned out that Ellen was not just thinking about Antonio's disfigurement, but also about something he did not expect.

"I think it should be clear. What mother would risk having disfigured children?"

"So, it wasn't the ugliness and the disfigurement in and of itself that repulsed her. She wasn't thinking of herself but about children! This is so unlike Gedda Lux's arguments and considerations! This is a much more sensible notion of marriage," Presto thought and said carelessly, "But they say he is very wealthy."

"There isn't enough money to pay for the grief of a mother whose children are miserable!" Ellen replied. "I can't stand here chatting with you, I haven't finished cleaning yet."

"Miss Ellen, may I come to the movies with you?"

"You may!" Ellen replied magnanimously from the back of the room.

The movie was *Presto the Cowboy* – one of his early directorial pieces.

As he sat in the dark cinema next to Ellen and gazed at the screen, Antonio remembered when this movie was filmed. Presto's name was already famous. Film studio owners tried to steal him from each other, reporters watched his every move. Sebastian, like a mean and incorruptible Cerberus, watched every door. Presto's employer did not allow any strangers on the lot. During one crowd scene with many extras dressed as cowboys, one clever reporter managed to ride into the forbidden zone in costume, and became lost in the crowd of extras. Then, using a break in filming, he got to Presto and tried to interview him. This trick amused Presto, but he still did not answer a single question. This did not prevent the enterprising reporter from publishing a long interview that was published in every newspaper. The interview contained all sorts of things! Antonio Presto's alleged engagement to a millionaire widow, Missus U.; a new contract offered to Mister Presto by a large movie studio, promising him the income three times that of the King of England; Presto's plans for a new movie script *Creation*, in which he planned to play Adam. This was all so ridiculous and wildly impossible, that Presto didn't even bother issuing a protest. But the American public, hungry for all manner of sensations, talked of nothing else for days. And now? Now he was nothing – *tabula rasa* – a blank slate. No one knew what was to be written on it.

The audience burst into laughter. Ellen laughed more than anyone else.

Did Presto do the right thing by changing his appearance? Or was it a fateful mistake? As Ellen rocked with laughter, her shoulder touched Antonio's shoulder. This touch made Presto become fully aware of his new body – young and healthy. There was no longer the wall of disfigurement standing between him and Ellen, or between him and all the women in the world, between him and the love he so needed in life. This was worth sacrificing a lot, even his fame. Fame by itself could not give as much happiness and enjoyment as love! And fame could be recaptured again. If only he could find his identity!

Even there, in the movie theater, he continued searching for his new path. Was he a comedian or a tragedian? Should he act to inspire laughter or tears? He felt he was hesitating between these two paths, undecided as to which one to choose. Complex and difficult work was taking place in his subconscious.

He came from the lower class. His childhood had been tough and hungry. He knew how fickle fate could be, how much a little man depended on the whims of the privileged few. All this created a series of unique sympathies and dislikes and led to a certain sequence of life events. Brief events and street scenes he observed, incidents and thoughts he read about in books flickered through his mind, dropped into the dark depths of his subconscious and was subject to processing and systematization. When he accumulated enough material, all these separate facts, thoughts, and impressions would merge into a cohesive whole, and come back to the surface of his mind as a fully formed decision.

That was exactly what happened to Presto by the end of the movie. He did not yet have all the details of his new idea, but the main part was in place. Yes, he found his new face! He was so moved and overjoyed, that he exclaimed like Archimedes when he discovered the law of displaced liquids, "Eureka! I got it!"

The movie theater was thundering with laughter, and Presto's exclamation drowned in the noise. Only his neighbor on the right glanced at him oddly, and Ellen asked, "Did you lose something and then find it?"

"Yes! All is well!" Presto replied and took a deep breath. "I found my specific weight," he said quietly.

The painful hesitations and ponderings of the new Buddha were over. He felt as if he was reborn. He was not afraid of any troubles he might encounter ahead.

"The end!" Ellen said regretfully when the screen faded to black.

"The beginning!" Presto replied merrily. He responded to Ellen's questioning gaze, "An Indian philosopher said that every end is always the beginning of something new."

On the way home, Antonio was uncommonly upbeat and jovial. Ellen noticed.

"I had no idea you were so funny," she said. "It's as if you are a different man or as if you found a full wallet."

"I am a new man, and I found a wallet!" Presto exclaimed. "Look, Ellen, such wonderful stars, what an amazing night!"

"Are you a poet as well?"

"Of course I am. Would you like me to write you a poem, Ellen? Would you like to be in the movies? Be an actress?"

"In the movies? I wouldn't even know which way to turn!" the girl laughed.

"What if you could be yourself? Actresses make a lot of money."

"No, I don't want to be an actress," Ellen replied. "They are all kind of twisted." And Ellen rolled her shoulders so comically, imitating the society lionesses that Antonio laughed.

"You must be the only woman in the world who doesn't want to be a movie actress. What do you want to be? Have you thought of your future?"

"What is there to think about? The future will come anyway," the girl replied. "Things will get better, Uncle John will find a job as a teacher again, I will get a job too."

"And then? Then I'll get married and have children."

"The same optimism of an average American! Poor thing! You will face many disappointments!" Presto thought and said, "May your wishes come true!"

A MYSTERIOUS FIND

Presto indeed seemed like a new man. Ellen watched her tenant in astonishment. In the past, Adam Smith spent his mornings sprawled in the grass under the pine tree or spent hours by the lake with his fishing rod. Presently, he became extremely energetic. In the morning he wrote many letters in his room or took down notes from books, and frequently went to the post office, where his mail was kept for pickup. In the last few days, his correspondence grew tremendously. The tenant returned from the post office with entire stacks of letters and newspapers. Once, while cleaning up his room, Ellen peeked at a sheet of paper on his desk out of curiosity and read, "There are 52,000 movie theaters in the world, with the total of 21 million seats.

"The money invested in these theaters – 11 billion gold marks, 60% of which is America's share.

"Investments into America's movie industry reach two billion dollars.

"Making a film costs from $200,000 to $40,000,000, sometimes higher.

"70 movies are made every year.

"Film production costs: actors' salaries – 25%, building rental – 20%, sets – 19%, salaries of directors, assistants, and cameramen – 10%, screen writer – 10%, outdoor filming – 8%, film – 5%, costumes – 5%.

"Weekly expenses of one film studio in Hollywood – several billion dollars per week, with 71 writers on staff, 31 directors, 49 stars, plus an army of extras and technical staff.

"Cost of one movie theater – over a million dollars.

"Banks own all the studios, Hollywood, and 27,000 movie theaters. The films are often censored through banks.

"10 million people go to movie theaters every day at the price of 25 cents to $2; opening nights – from $2 up.

"Newspaper advertisement - $5,000,000.

"P.S. Some of these numbers are outdated. Must check for new information."

Ellen had no time to read more, and she wasn't all that interested. Mister Smith must have been writing something about cinema.

Another time, Ellen found an envelope Antonio accidentally forgot on the desk. The envelope was addressed to the local post office to be picked up by Mister Antonio Presto.

Ellen was surprised by this. The famous Antonio Presto was still alive and, apparently, living somewhere nearby. But how did the open envelope end up on Mister Smith's desk? This was the puzzle. Perhaps, Mister Smith was a relative or close friend of Antonio Presto. It occurred to Ellen that there was some elusive similarity between Antonio Presto, whom she knew from screen, and their tenant, despite the fact that Smith was a normal, healthy young man, and Presto was a freak. Ellen was extremely interested in her discovery. But she didn't dare talk about it either to her uncle or to her tenant. She couldn't admit to her immodest curiosity and reading someone else's papers. The aura of mystery added a new level of interest to Mister Smith in Ellen's eyes. Until then, she considered Smith a modest journalist, down on his luck, who didn't even have the means to stay at a hotel. And now it turned out that he had a very close and mysterious connection with Antonio Presto himself. Maybe that was why Smith decided to live at the park ranger's modest home. She started watching the tenant with so much attention, that he finally noticed and asked her, "Ellen, you don't take your eyes off me lately. Are you in love?"

The girl was taken aback, then became a little angry and replied, "Not at all. You are imagining."

"What am I imagining? That you are in love with me? I am not insisting on that. But it's a fact that you keep watching me in a peculiar way."

"Just you wait, I'll give you an answer!" Ellen thought and said, "Perhaps you are right. The thing is, you remind me of Antonio Presto."

It was Presto's turn to be taken aback. "Did she read the address on the envelope? I may have left it on the desk once. No, she wouldn't have. Ellen has too little interest in me to read my papers."

"Indeed!" Presto exclaimed, regaining control. "You remind me of an old lady friend of mine – you are a spitting image of her. You have a great imagination. You might even imagine that I am Antonio Presto himself."

Ellen laughed and exclaimed, "My imagination is not that great. Such miracles are impossible."

Presto sighed with relief, but became more thoughtful and cautious in his conversations with Ellen.

His mood has changed again. He was clearly nervous. He went to the post office even more frequently. Ellen frequently heard him pacing around the room. He almost stopped coming out into the garden.

In those days he was waiting for the final answer on his case from Piers, the attorney. Piers has already informed Presto that after the governor, the prosecutor, and other participants of the farewell dinner had to use Doctor Zorn's assistance to change their appearance, the legislative proposal for stripping such people of their property rights had been withdrawn. The entire plan was devised by the clever Piers. His agents also delivered Zorn's miraculous powders using the mysterious methods of their own, possibly including bribes to Zorn's servants.

"I had no doubt that they would withdraw the proposal," Piers wrote. "This way, we have removed the biggest obstacle, and all we have to do now is formally establish the connection of your new persona with the old Presto. This will not be difficult. It is a victory that the court recognized the power of attorney you gave me, and thus acknowledged your mental capacity and your rights."

Piers proceeded to use his influence and connections to get a court date as soon as possible, to make sure "there were no stumbling blocks."

Finally the day arrived that would become very memorable for Presto and Ellen.

A MOMENTOUS DAY

In the morning, while Ellen was in the kitchen, a postman arrived and said, "A telegram for Mister Antonio Presto."

Ellen looked at him in astonishment and replied, "Antonio Presto doesn't live here."

The postman shrugged, looked at the telegram, and held it out to Ellen.

"This is the right address. See for yourself."

Ellen looked at the address.

"Yes," she said, "this is our address, but Antonio Presto doesn't live here. It must be a mistake." And she handed the telegram back to the postman.

The postman took it, shrugged again, and left.

Presto saw him through the window and called out, "Hello! Who is the telegram for?"

"Antonio Presto," the postman said.

"Give it here. I am Antonio Presto."

The postman walked to the window, looking puzzled.

"But," he hesitated, "I was told that Antonio Presto didn't live here. And besides, if that's the same Antonio Presto everyone knows, then you don't look much like him, Mister." The postman kept turning the telegram over and over in his hands.

"Come, come!" Presto exclaimed impatiently, reaching for the telegram. "You have delivered the telegram at the correct address, and I am the recipient, what else do you want?"

"But the young lady said…" the postman was still reluctant.

Presto snatched the telegram from his hands, opened it and read, "Court decided in your favor. Congratulations. Piers."

"Excellent," Presto said happily. "Don't worry. You have delivered the telegram to the right person. Let me sign for it. And here is for the delivery and for good news." And Presto handed the postman the receipt along with ten dollars.

The postman beamed, thanked him, wished him all the best, and marched back to the post office.

"Victory!" Presto exclaimed, beside himself, shook the telegram over his head, made a dance move, turned, and saw Ellen standing in the doorway of his room with her eyes wide with astonishment and her face pale.

"Why did you do that?" she asked dully.

"Did you see and hear everything? What did I do, Miss Ellen?"

"Why did you take the telegram sent to Antonio Presto? Why did you lie to the postman?"

"I did not lie to him, and I took the telegram because I am Antonio Presto."

"That's impossible."

"Nevertheless, it is a fact!" Presto exclaimed merrily.

"Then you deceived us – my uncle and me – by calling yourself Mister Smith."

"Yes, guilty as charged. Certain circumstances forced me to do this. Please do not condemn me before you get my explanation. When Mister Barry returns from his rounds, I shall tell you everything."

Ellen went back to the kitchen without another word, looking glum. This was too strange and turned all her notions about their tenant upside down. She wouldn't have dared to say to Presto much of what she said to Smith. She recalled all their conversations and how stern she sometimes was with the down-on-his-luck reporter. Then she started consoling herself, "No, it can't be the famous Antonio Presto from the movies. He must be a namesake, maybe a relative." She was so overcome with doubt and curiosity that she could barely do anything right that day.

When she showed up in Presto's room with a mop and a rag in one hand and a bucket of water in another, she looked very awkward. How was she to treat this new Presto? She didn't say, "Get out and stay out of my way!" as she normally would, but looked at him almost guiltily and stammered, "Mister...Presto! Would you mind going to the garden?"

"Right away!" Presto replied. "One moment..." He was quickly writing something on a telegraph form.

This minor delay made Ellen angry. She thought that Presto was purposely stalling and taking on airs. She was angry at herself too! It was as if she was groveling before him! She said with her usual sternness, "I have to clean!"

"All done!" Presto said. "Forgive me for being in your way. With your permission, I won't go to the garden, but to the post office. Pip!" he called the dog. "Let's go for a walk!"

The St. Bernard, who has long since been peeking into the room, barked happily, and jumped up. Presto left.

"Mister Sm… Mister Presto!" Ellen called out to him despite herself. Her curiosity got the better of her.

Presto turned.

"Forgive me," she said and her cheeks turned crimson. "Just tell me one thing, before my uncle returns, are you the same Antonio Presto… or not?"

"Both," he replied. "Pardon me, I am really in a rush to get to the post office. Be patient."

He left accompanied by Pip.

Ellen stood there, deep in thought, leaning on the mop, and then started cleaning fiercely.

But the events of this memorable day were not over yet.

Piers usually sent all of Presto's correspondence care of the made-up Smith, as they agree. He sent the last telegram to Antonio Presto at the park ranger's house, assuming that Presto no longer needed to remain incognito. The telegram itself, with the full address and his real name intended to symbolize that the new Presto was a full and acknowledged heir to the rights of the old Presto. Such a telegram couldn't help but please the client. Piers was right in that. But the lawyer did not think of all the consequences of his actions.

Reporters from the largest newspapers have long since tried to determine the location of the new Presto after he disappeared so suddenly. It was a kind of sport to them. Everyone wanted to be the first to find him. They had their own paid agents among the post office employees, who would inform them immediately should anything of interest occur.

Before Presto returned from the post office, a car with one such omnipresent reporter rolled up to Barry's house. He was living in a nearby hotel and received a telegram from his agent from the New York post office that a telegram has been dispatched to Antonio Presto, with a Yellowstone address. This happened an hour before Presto received his telegram. The reporter left immediately.

He looked like a prosperous salesman. He could be mistaken for a tourist. Two cameras hung from the straps crisscrossing his chest – a small kinematic one and an SLR. Even before he stepped out of his car, he managed to photograph the park ranger's house and Ellen, peeking out of the window with a mop in her hands. In a few minutes, he took several dozen shots and bustled about with courteous unceremoniousness. He drowned a blushing Ellen in questions. The girl was so taken aback, that she replied in single syllables, but in the meantime, the journalist filled page after page with stenographic hieroglyphs. But when the unexpected guest walked up to Presto's desk, clearly intending to examine his papers, Ellen lost her temper. All of her anger against the annoying visitor suddenly broke through. She stepped between him and the desk like a sentinel, hefted her mop and said in a voice halting with anxiety, "Mister! The master is not at home. Please leave his room this instant!"

"He-he! What a firecracker you are!" Mistaking Ellen for a daughter or a maid of a poor ranger, he pulled out his fat wallet and counted off a few bills. "Perhaps, you will be a bit kinder, if…"

"Out!" Ellen shouted, swinging the mop in front of the reporter's face.

Taken aback, he mumbled, "Come now…" and staggered out of the room backwards under Ellen's supervision.

"What will happen now?" Ellen thought, sensing that she may have gone too far. How would Presto react if the reporter complained to him about her actions?

Suddenly she heard Pip's barking and sighed as if she dropped a heavy load off her back.

"Mister Presto can deal with him as he pleases."

Mister Presto's approach was very simple.

"No interviews, go away!" he said firmly. Presto was used to dealing with reporters.

The journalist realized immediately that this was a hopeless matter. All he could do was angrily click his camera a few more times, to photograph the newly found Presto. But the latter was as quick as a lizard and turned his back before the lens cover was removed.

The car left. Presto found Ellen frozen in the doorway, with the mop still in her hands.

"Did this scoundrel cause you any trouble?" Presto asked kindly.

"Yes, but I think I repaid him in kind," Ellen replied and, unable to contain her agitation, told Presto everything.

Antonio laughed and bowed.

"You did a splendid job protecting my interests, Miss. However, it's vexing! Now the reporters will descend like locusts. I shall tell Piers off for his carelessness. They will force me out of the house. Although, I was planning to leave soon, and there is much I have to discuss with you and your uncle before my departure. Look, if someone shows up, tell them I went to Canada. Don't be shy, if you have to, use your triumphant mop."

Indeed, there were several more reporter attacks that day, but Ellen showed them out vigorously, purposely assuming the role of a coarse, illiterate, stupid woman. Presto, who was hiding in the garden, observed these scenes and whispered, "I wish Hoffman was here with his camera! It's alright! We'll have a chance to film her in this role!"

In the evening, when Barry returned, Presto told his unusual story to the ranger scientist and his niece over dinner. Ellen hung on his every word.

"What are you planning to do next?" Barry asked when Presto finished his story.

"I already have a plan, which I created under your roof. No one knows about it yet, and I would like for it to remain between us for now. It's obvious from my story that even the greatest actors depend entirely on the moneymakers," Presto continued. "Mister Pitch rejected me. Very well! We'll see who gets the last laugh. I will try to do without the likes of him."

"Do you intend to join the Screen Actors' Guild? I heard they were starting their own enterprise," Barry asked.

"Screen Actors' Guild is only the first attempt of the film industry workers to protect their own interests," Presto replied. "But, essentially, it's an association of movie stars. It is saturated with the spirit of commerce, and the supporting actors, let alone the extras, don't have a very good time of it. Besides, even as part of the guild, I would not be entirely free from the creative standpoint. And I need complete freedom – freedom to write screenplays, to direct, and to act. I can tell in advance that what I am planning to do in this area is not going to be to the guild's liking."

"Based on this, you are planning to set up your own film studio," Barry said.

"Exactly."

Barry said nothing, but raised his eyebrow, puffed on his pipe and exhaled a stream of smoke.

"Do you doubt my success?" Presto asked and continued without waiting for an answer, "I believe in it. Mister Pitch's lawsuit, my treatment and, most importantly the trial, have very much undermined my finances. Still, I have enough to begin. At the very least, enough to produce the first picture. And then? Of course, I cannot count on loans. The banks will consider my enterprise dangerous and not only refuse to loan me money but also get in my way. I can anticipate that. But I am counting on something else. My enterprise is not going to be strictly commercial, although, of course, it must not lose money, otherwise I won't be able to continue the struggle. It will be cooperative in nature, much more so than the Screen Actors' Guild. It won't just be a community of actors, but all other workers involved, down to the last carpenter and janitor. Hollywood alone always has over a hundred unemployed directors and thousands of actors. They will happily agree to be paid less at first, until the enterprise brings profit, from which they all will benefit. But I don't think I will have to impose such restrictions. On the contrary, I will try to provide significantly better conditions for the low- and middle-level workers. Collaboration based on the unity of our interests will allow us to win the struggle even against the Leviathans of the movie industry. At least, this is my hope."

"It's up to you," Barry said.

"I am betting on people," Presto continued enthusiastically. "I need faithful helpers, who understand me and whom I can rely on. And so I thought of you, Mister Barry."

"Me?" Barry replied in surprise.

"Yes, you and Miss Ellen. This backwater, albeit the most picturesque backwater in the world, is not a place for you, an intelligent and educated man. It's also not a place for Miss Ellen. I am offering you to leave your job as a ranger and come work for me. I can guarantee that your initial salary will be twice what you used to earn as a teacher."

"But I know nothing of the movie industry!" Barry objected.

"That is why you are so surprised by my proposal. But the movie industry is vast and complex, with all manner of jobs within it. For starters, I have work for you that any literate man can handle. For instance, in the contract department. When you become better acquainted with the industry, you will be able to assume a more responsible post, up to a manager, complete with a very respectable salary. There will also be work for Miss Ellen."

"As long as it's not acting!" the girl said quickly.

"The choice of work will depend entirely on you," Antonio rushed to reassure her.

"This is all very unexpected," Barry said, clearly hesitating.

Presto understood his doubts – this was a man who already had his fair share of failures. He was afraid to lose what little he had.

"I have told you honestly," Presto tried convincing him again, "that this enterprise is risky to me personally. My risk is greater than yours. I don't think you are risking all that much. In a year or two with me you will earn more than you could in ten years at your current job. You will acquire new skills, and, thus, new opportunities to move on without me."

Barry still hesitated. Then Antonio decided to use his weakness. He already knew how much John loved his niece, and how upset he was that this intelligent, capable girl was stuck here, in the sticks, without education or future.

"Think of Miss Ellen!" Presto exclaimed. "Why should she spend the rest of her life with mops and pans?"

"Don't worry about me!" Ellen blushed. "I am not complaining and am happy with my lot."

"But you could be happier," Presto objected. "You will be in a new society, where you can meet interesting, well-educated people."

"I am happy here," the girl replied glumly.

"Stubborn girl! I hope she doesn't ruin everything!" Presto thought in frustration. If only she and her uncle knew the true reason for Presto's eloquence! If only Ellen could guess, that she was the crux of the matter, that Antonio's hopes in his new work were associated with her!

Presto's words about Ellen, and her last answer, filled with unwilling sadness, made an impression with Barry. Giving up, he said, "You must understand, Mister Presto, it is difficult for me to leave a safe spot, even if I wanted to. I have nothing to hide from you. I have no savings to move or rent an apartment."

"It's nothing!" Presto exclaimed optimistically, already anticipating victory. "I can give you an advance today. Enough for a move, an apartment, and for settling down. Besides, you won't need to rent an apartment. I inherited from the old Presto a very nice, spacious villa, where I live alone. The entire top floor is empty. You can live there with your niece. I will be happy to have you. I have grown accustomed to you, and we have become friends."

"I thank you for your kindness, but that would be awkward. Extremely awkward," Barry replied.

"Why?" Presto asked, but then guessed the answer. "Yes, of course. Public opinion. I am a bachelor, and there are no women in my house. But that is nonsense, Mister Barry! First of all, Miss Ellen won't live alone but with you. You won't even be on the same floor. Why couldn't I rent out the top floor of my own house? Besides, we could find a companion for Miss Ellen, some respectable old lady. And then none of our bigots and hypocrites will have anything to complain about. Well then, do we have a deal?"

"Deal!" Barry replied.

Ellen blushed through her dark tan. Her eyes sparkled. She could no longer contain her joy and asked with childish impatience, addressing both Presto and her uncle, "When are we leaving?"

HOME AGAIN

Presto arrived at his house ahead of Barry and Ellen. The ranger had to stay behind for a few days to finish his business with the park's management and sell what he couldn't take with him.

Presto's return took place in a fairly formal setting. A court official and a lawyer, one of Piers' associates, were present during his "reestablishment on property."

Pointing at Presto, the official said to Sebastian who opened the door, "This young man is your master, Antonio Presto, who changed his appearance. He is the rightful owner of this house, and you must treat him accordingly and fulfill his orders."

Sebastian bowed glumly and let the visitors in.

The official and the lawyer went through all the rooms, marveling at the treasures of art Presto collected with the strict and sophisticated taste of a connoisseur. After a lively breakfast, the official and the lawyer left.

"I am home!" Presto exclaimed, happily stretching out in an armchair. A familiar footstool was still nearby, but he no longer needed it.

There was a knock on the door.

"Come in!"

Sebastian appeared in the doorway. He was very embarrassed. His white eyebrows were drawn together, and his sagging lips moved silently. Presto decided to help him out and asked jovially, "Well, what have you been doing here without me, Sebastian?"

The old servant sighed, but remained silent. Presto laughed.

"I see you still can't get used to my new look."

"Mister Presto!" Sebastian finally said, then halted, as if he ran out of breath.

"Well?"

"Allow me to leave your employment."

"Leave? Why? You want to leave me?" Presto asked, surprised. "You, my old faithful servant, who took care of me for so many years, as if I were a child?"

Sebastian shrugged and replied with a sad smile, "But you were a child. Or almost like a child. And now you are all grown up and you don't need a nanny."

There was a lot of tenderness in the heart of this severe-looking old man. He did view Presto as a child, became attached to him, and truly took care of him like a devoted nanny. Presto knew about it and was, in turn, very fond of the old man.

"But my dear fellow!" Presto exclaimed, rising from the armchair and walking up to Sebastian. "Were my needs limited to needing help with a footstool, or with things I couldn't reach because of my small height? You managed my entire household, you were my right hand."

Sebastian sighed again and frowned even more.

"But I can't remain in this house after what happened," he replied.

"And what happened exactly?" Presto asked. "The fact that you didn't want to let me into the house?"

"And set up an ambush, and handed you to the police, and insulted you," Sebastian continued. "Such things cannot be forgotten, and I don't want you to fire me in disgrace because of them sooner or later. I'd rather leave on my own."

"What an oddball you are!" Presto said heatedly. "Listen, Sebastian! I promise you, that I do not blame you at all and I am not angry. Of course, I didn't enjoy it. But you acted exactly as any honest servant should. I would have done the same thing in your place. Let us forget it all and be friends as before."

Sebastian's wrinkled face grew slightly more cheerful, but his eyebrows were still drawn together.

"You only think you can forget," he said.

"Not at all!" Presto objected and gently placed his hands onto Sebastian's shoulders. Now their faces were on the same level. In the past Presto used to look up at his servant, as he did with everyone else.

"There really is something in this face resembling my little Presto," the old man said, looking at Presto's new face for the first time.

"Then you are… really Presto?" Sebastian asked.

"Of course," Antonio replied with a smile. "Do you still doubt it?"

"Forgive me, but I am a simple man, and my mind boggles when I think about all this. And I think, what if some look-alike scoundrel killed my boy and declared himself to be Presto. And now I have to serve him."

"So, that's the problem! I think you have finally made your point. Come with me!"

Presto walked over to the desk, showed Sebastian the entire series of photographs portraying all phases of transformation of the old Presto into the new one, and explained why and how it happened. Sebastian was overwhelmed. He shook his head and sorted through the photos, comparing them to Presto's current face.

"It's a miracle!" he finally exclaimed.

"Yes, a miracle of science," Presto said. "Do you believe me now, when I say I am not some criminal who killed your little boy? And if you still don't, I can tell you everything that has happened since you came to my house, all our conversations, every detail. There isn't a single criminal, no matter how deft, who could know all that!" Presto reminded him of a few incidents that no one else knew about. Only then did the old man smile a sincere smile and exclaimed, "Then my boy really did grow up!"

"There you go! All is well, old man!" Presto exclaimed. "Are we back to normal?"

Sebastian nodded.

"This was one of my hardest won victories," Presto thought and continued, "And there you were, trying to leave when I need you most. More than never. I am beginning a new life, Sebastian. Incidentally, what do you think, what sort of furniture we might need to furnish a room for a young woman? Dressing tables, chest of drawers, a mirror?"

Sebastian smiled just with his eyes, "So that's the turn his new life is taking! Well, why not – since he is all grown up!"

An observant Presto didn't miss the merry flicker in the eyes of his old servant.

"Don't think that I am planning to bring a wife into the house," Presto rushed to explain. "No, it's just that I decided to rent out the rooms in the top floor. What do I need them for? A gentleman and his niece will be staying there. I am renting the rooms complete with furniture."

"Are things really that bad?" Sebastian asked with concern.

"What do you mean?"

"Did all these judges and lawyers bleed you dry, so that you are having to rent rooms? I have been reading the papers."

"No, Sebastian, things are not quite that bad. But you see, my tenant will be working for me as my secretary. I am starting my own company. I need for him to be nearby. And he has a niece."

"I see!" Sebastian said meaningfully. And added in his mind, "Still, if the niece is involved, something is going on here." With all the sincerity of an old nanny, he asked, "So this niece? She is a young woman, you said? Very young?"

"Yes."

"Would she be alright in a bachelor's house, even with her uncle?"

"Not him too! He is the second person to mention this, and, probably, not the last!" Presto thought, mentally cursing hypocritical society standards. Ellen's living at his house could easily provide food for rumors. But he wouldn't give up, and Ellen was not the kind of girl to pay attention to such nonsense!

"You are right, Sebastian. But I have thought about this. We should find a companion for the young lady. A middle-aged woman from good society. And then everything will be alright."

Sebastian nodded, and they started making a list of furniture and other necessities for the new tenants.

THE NEW SANCHO PANZA

"Turn! Again! Walk! Sit! Rise! A gesture of surprise… horror… sudden joy."

Presto was standing in the middle of a large room with northern exposure. One wall and part of the roof were glass. All other walls were draped with black velvet. There was a black square in the middle of the parquet floor – the focus point of a movie camera. This was Antonio's home studio. Hoffman stood a few paces away from him, looking through the camera. He had captured many of Presto's effective poses and gestures in this room, having spent days observing the unique dwarf. Presently, Hoffman was studying the new Presto.

"That's enough for today. We still have much to discuss, Hoffman!" Presto said and, stepping out of the "magic" square, walked over to the glass wall, where there was a table and two armchairs. The table was piled with folders of documents, a cigar case, a box of cigarettes, a lighter, and an ashtray.

Antonio lit a cigarette.

"Well?" he asked Hoffman with some anxiety.

Hoffman unhurriedly cut the tip of a cigar with an automatic cutter, lit it, exhaled a stream of smoke, and finally replied, looking off to the side.

"I am not seeing your new face yet, Presto. You have gained much but also lost much. Your movements have become slower and smoother. This is a good innovation. Remember how much trouble you used to cause me with your quick, fidgety movements? We had to make exceptions for you because, first of all, you couldn't help it, and second, this was one of the unique characteristics of your artistic persona. Still, I often had to film you in slow motion, while making your fellow actors speed up their movements a little, to find a balance. It was hellishly difficult work. Now, this challenge no longer exists. But what is new? I can't feel it yet. To be honest, if you came to the studio for a screen test, as an unknown young man wanting to try becoming a movie actor, I am not sure whether a producer, a cameraman, or a director would be interested in you."

Presto discarded his cigarette, as if it was too bitter, and lit a cigar.

"Forgive me for being so honest…" Hoffman said awkwardly.

"Honesty is the best approach," Presto replied. "I won't deny that your words upset me a little, but they do not surprise me. I expected this. It couldn't be any other way. But I believe in myself. My new face! It's not enough to twirl in front of you to really see it. You know my creative method. I must get into a role, reinvent myself as my hero, live through his life, all his thoughts and feelings, and then the necessary gestures, facial expressions, and poses will emerge on their own and uncover the face. Just wait. I am already working on a screenplay. When I appear as my new hero, you will see my new face."

"What is the screenplay about?" Hoffman asked.

Presto frowned, and Hoffman laughed.

"I see there is still much left in you from the old Presto!" he exclaimed. "Every new screenplay was a mystery to everyone, until you put down the last period. Ooh, how cantankerous you used to be during that time! It was as if you were obsessed. You were impossible to talk to. You either became irritated or gazed vacantly at the other person. You stopped sleeping and eating, like someone badly ill. But then, one day, you showed up smiling happily and became kind and engaging. And everyone at the studio – from the stars to the carpenters – knew: the new screenplay was ready!"

Presto smiled and replied, "Yes, it's true. I don't think I've changed in this respect."

"If you don't want to tell me about the new screenplay, could you at least introduce me to your general plans? As I understand, your new face should create a new direction in your work."

"It can't be any other way," Presto said and reached out for one of the folders. "This is what I wanted to talk to you about."

Antonio rummaged through the folder and pulled out a sheet of paper.

"Here, how do you like this excerpt from Walt Whitman, 'You must admit, that to a perceptive eye all these cities, swarming with miserable grotesques, cripples, senselessly aping jokers, and freaks, must look like some sort of a boring desert. In the shops, in the streets, in the churches, in the pubs, in the public places – everywhere you look there is carelessness, shallowness, deceit and lies; foppish, weak, vain, prematurely ripe youth; excessive lust, unhealthy bodies – male and female, made up and disguised, with fake hair, dirty complexion and bad blood. Capacity for motherhood is expiring or has already expired, and there are vulgar notions of beauty, low morals, or rather, complete absence of morals on the scale unseen anywhere else in the world.' This was

Whitman's description of American democracy in his day. You must agree, that presently the outlook is not better, but worse," Presto concluded.

Hoffman listened to him carefully, first with surprise, then with increasing alarm, and finally with disdain.

"What do you think?" Presto asked.

"You want to take this perilous path?" Hoffman asked with horror.

"Why perilous?"

"The path of uncovering social injustice? The path of politics? Do you want to challenge the national pride? You will be trampled! Everyone with power and money will turn against you. And the viewers will turn away from you too – because they will not enjoy being a patient under the scalpel of an angry surgeon."

"Don't get so excited, Hoffman! Listen to me."

But Hoffman continued, like a priest accusing a sinner, "Remember the fate of the films by the director Erich von Stroheim. He didn't want to make 'happy' movies. And what happened? They were received coldly despite all their artistic virtues."

"Then we must make certain that my films are received with admiration," Presto objected. "Don't think that I am planning to create coarsely propagandist films showing garrets and basements, horrors of exploitation and unemployment. I want to create the kind of movies that would make people laugh no less, and possibly more than before. I want to show beauty and grandeur of the soul where no one had seen it before. You and I have seen much, Hoffman. You have no idea how much grace and elegance there is in the simple movements of a girl cleaning a room or hanging laundry. We have filmed too many palaces and aristocrats. Don't be afraid. There will be ceaseless laughter at my movies. Laughter and tears. After all, the audience likes to cry sometimes. You know this. The viewers will leave the movie theater enthralled. And in one or two days, they will start thinking. Unnoticeably to themselves, they will arrive at the conclusion that our world and our famous democracy are not all that great, that we have to find another way, and not just stubbornly believe in the return of the golden age that is gone forever. This is my goal!

"I am telling you all this honestly, Hoffman," Presto said after a pause. "But for the spectators, and our entire so-called society, will probably take some time to figure out the 'social craftiness' of my new movies."

"They will figure it out! And sooner than you think!" Hoffman disagreed. "Mister Pitch will be the first one to reject your screenplays. If not him, then the censors at Bank of New York, on whom he depends, will slice it, dice it, and 'correct' it – and that is the best case scenario. In the worst case, they will refuse to grant you a release."

"I don't need one," Presto said.

"I don't understand you."

"It shouldn't be hard to understand. I am starting my own studio."

Hoffman leaned back in his chair and exclaimed, "It's worse than I thought! This is madness! I know you have some capital. But your means are but a stick against a canon. Everyone will declare war on you – the banks, their light cavalry – the press, the movie rentals, the cinema owners. Pitch spends millions every week, and his company is not the wealthiest in Hollywood. You are headed toward certain bankruptcy, Presto, and I feel sorry for you. I thought Presto the dwarf was a practical man."

Antonio smiled.

"Time will tell, whether the old or the new Presto is more practical. Don't think that I am acting rashly, Hoffman." He patted the folders. "We will look into this material later, and you shall see that I have foreseen everything. No matter what happens, the risk is all mine. I will invite only a few major actors. If I go bankrupt, they will always find other work. I plan to hire the supporting actors, the extras, and other staff from unemployed union members. At worst, this will be a breather for them."

"And what if major actors refuse to work with you? After all, Miss Lux is not going to play a laundress!"

"I will manage without them," Presto replied. "What I really cannot do without right now is an experienced, talented cameraman. But I am counting on you, Hoffman. Will you, my old friend, denounce me and say, 'I don't know him'?"

A strained pause followed. Hoffman exhaled smoke rings, deep in thought. Then he said, as if thinking out loud, "My job is small – to run the camera. But still, I do care what I film. By working with you, I shall transfer into the camp opposing the banks and be labeled 'red'. And the banks will take revenge on me. If you go bankrupt, I will have problems finding another job."

Presto could not help but agree with this argument, and so he did not object, but anxiously waited to hear the refusal. Hoffman paused again, watching the smoke rings.

"But I also don't want to leave you, old man, at this difficult time. You are doing something prodigiously stupid. It's perfectly clear to me. And then you ask me to help you go bankrupt faster…"

"Actually, without you, I would crash even sooner, Hoffman. But that is not the point. Please understand, I began this lopsided battle first of all in the interests of the movie industry workers themselves."

Presto spoke passionately about the ruthless exploitation of the film workers by the entrepreneurs, about the lawlessness, the suppression of rights, the talentless 'stars' talked up by the publicity, the hopeless position of the talented youth.

Hoffman was very familiar with all this, having been through many a hard experience himself.

"It is time to change this intolerable situation," Presto concluded. "My dream is that of cooperation and collaborative protection of the workers' interests. We don't yet realize our own power."

"But we realize very well the power of our enemies," Hoffman replied sedately.

"*He will refuse,*" Presto thought sadly. But Hoffman simply continued puffing out smoke rings.

Presto was his friend, but he also had to look after himself. It was precisely because Hoffman had a rough past that he did not want to risk what he had. But was the risk all that great? If the new Presto turned out to be a poor actor and his screenplays had "dangerous thoughts," Hoffman would know about it before the film made it to the big screen and would be able to leave. He could even make it look like a protest and protect his reputation.

Hoffman smiled and said, "You are a Don Quixote, Presto. And every Don Quixote ought to have his own Sancho Panza. Well, why don't you take me on as your squire, oh noble knight of La Mancha, although we won't be fighting any windmills!"

Presto firmly shook his friend's hand.

"Together, we shall conquer all the giants, my dear Hoffman, and I appoint you the island governor in advance!" he exclaimed.

"You, Don Quixote, are nothing but trouble," the new Sancho Panza sighed. "Thank you for the honor. I am not certain whether we shall capture an island, but there are bound to be a lot of beatings to befall our heads."

"We shall retaliate, Hoffman. In the meantime, let us ready for the battle."

He opened the folders filled with notes and calculations he made by the shore of the Emerald Lake and started introducing Hoffman to his plans.

THE STRUGGLE BEGINS

Presto became very busy. He rented a large building where he set up a temporary office. The place was crowded from morning until night with the staff and actors applying for jobs and contracts being signed. The news of a new film studio spread quickly among the Hollywood unemployed. Actors, extras, workers of all specialties came in droves and lined up in long queues. Presto himself received every candidate, including the extras, talked to them, made them pose and act in improvised scenes. Whatever his challenges were, there was no lack of people. At four in the afternoon, the interviews of actors and staff ended and, after a quick meal, Presto moved on to other business matters – talking to realtors about purchasing or leasing a plot of land for building the movie studio as well as meeting with contractors, suppliers and architects.

This second portion of the day was much more difficult for Presto than the first. Not only the jobless but also the film industry producers became aware of the new enterprise. They couldn't help but worry about the new competitor. Mister Pitch was particularly concerned – Antonio who was his trump card for the longest time, was now becoming his most dangerous rival. Pitch and other entrepreneurs started developing a strategy against Presto. Pitch sent his spies to Presto under the guise of the unemployed workers looking for jobs, lured away the most talented performers, and otherwise interfered as much as possible.

Antonio was prepared for all this. But it wasn't easy. For instance, his realtors located a suitable plot for the studio, all negotiations with the owner were complete, and all they had to do was close the deal. But Pitch found out about it at the last moment, and snatched up the plot by paying twice the original price for it.

Presto himself had to use trickery and deceit.

"When Barry gets here, he can buy a plot in his name, pretending it's for a farm or a garden. No one knows him yet, and I can trust him," Presto thought.

His competitors were particularly interested in what sort of movies Presto was planning to make. But despite all their tricks, they failed. As for the reporters, Antonio either refused to talk to them or started making up such nonsense that even the seasoned newspaper pirates were overwhelmed and didn't dare put such interviews into print. The actors who were excessively and suspiciously curious were told, "You will find out when we get to filming."

A disappointed Pitch met with Lux and said, "I am counting on your help, Ma'am."

"What's the matter?" she asked.

"The matter is," Pitch replied, "that this Antonio Presto is causing me trouble. He is positively refusing to take off his mask and show us his new face. What is he planning? What movies is he going to make? This is extremely important to me. Of course he is not going to make any historic pictures with castles, pyramids and thousands of extras. It's too expensive for him. And he was never interested in the outward effects. In all likelihood, Presto will use the cheap outdoor filming or use simple interiors. But the content! The content!"

Pitch paused.

"What do you want from me?" Lux asked, tired of waiting.

Pitch ignored her question and continued, seemingly thinking out loud.

"I want to have reliable information from Presto himself. I have sent a few people to him with a hint that if he came to me, he would receive a very interesting proposal. We not only wanted to know his plans, but also buy him back, if possible. The banks would lend us a significant sum, which might prove irresistible to him."

"What would you do with him if this deal took place?"

"At worst, I would freeze him, like any new invention threatening old established enterprises."

"You would pay him enormous money and keep him from acting? He would never agree."

"People agree to anything for the right amount," Pitch replied confidently. "Although if he managed to inspire a new kind of interest, contrary to expectations, we could control him and make him take the roles and act in screen plays we create."

"And what about Presto?"

"This obstinate mule refused to come to me. All that is left is to discover his plans, at the very least, and you must help me do this. He used to be in love with you and probably still is. He refused to see me, but he will probably come to you if you invite him. Of course, you did have a falling out. But women know how to play our kind at will," Pitch said with a sigh, recalling how much this feminine skill had cost him.

Lux thought about it. She herself didn't mind meeting with Presto. Of course, he rejected him both in his old and in his new guise. But much had changed since then. After all, Pitch also rejected the new Presto, and here he was, sending his ambassadors to him.

Lux has recently broken up with her fiancé, when she came to know him better. He exercised his rights of the future husband too soon and too strongly, clearly making a beeline for Lux's money, and she knew how to keep control of it. Also, Lux couldn't help but acknowledge that the new Presto was a very handsome man, no worse than Lorenzo. Finally, he was starting his own company, which, in case of success, could bring significant revenues. Once again, he was becoming a man with a future. Of course, this future was still unclear, and Lux was a careful and calculating woman. She had no plans, as of yet, of entering even into a business relationship with Presto. But he was worth keeping an eye on.

To elevate her actions in Pitch's eyes, Lux said, "You are putting me in a somewhat difficult position, Mister Pitch. It is not easy for me to appeal to Presto after what happened between us, and he nearly killed me. Still, I shall try to meet with him and fulfill your wishes."

"You are a smart girl and will do great!" Pitch exclaimed.

These words increased Presto's appeal in Lux's eyes – Pitch was very stingy with praises and compliments and only offered them in exceptional cases.

THE LOST ADMIRER

When a man is surrounded by enemies, he is bound to become suspicious and cautious despite himself. Having received and read Lux's letter, Antonio instantly guessed it to be another one of Pitch's tricks. However, he didn't mind seeing Lux again. He was still interested in her. He would have to be extra-cautious for that very reason. Of course, Lux would ask about his plans. Was there any need to keep them secret? Rehearsals would begin soon, and it would all become common knowledge anyway.

"Let Lux imagine that I couldn't resist her charms and melted like Samson before Delilah. Let's see how she reacts to my plans!" Presto thought.

On the appointed day and hour, Presto entered the familiar boudoir covered with rugs and furnished with ottomans, poofs and armchairs. It was colorful and eclectic. But the lady of the house who picked out these furnishings had her own considerations – when sitting or reclining in the armchairs and on settees, she could show off the most effective poses and demonstrate her "wares" to the best advantage, so to speak. This was very important, because it raised her value in the eyes of producers and directors coming to visit the star. Her beauty was her main treasure.

Lux received Presto dressed as Cleopatra, stretched on a long Egyptian divan with carved legs. Cleopatra was her new role, and Lux was accustomed to "adopting the new image" by transforming into her new heroine at home.

"I must feel like the Queen of Egypt," she said, sometimes even forcing her maid to wear the costume of an Egyptian slave girl and serve her chocolate in an Egyptian cup. In truth, this was more of a whim in hopes of creating a greater effect, rather than serious creative work.

Presto glanced at the new Cleopatra and felt none of his former turmoil. Despite the fact that Lux was dazzling in this exotic dress, he remained cold. He even imagined that he was faced with a wax statue instead of a living person.

Lux bestowed upon the guest one of her most irresistible smiles from her vast arsenal for anything her life and work had to offer.

"I am very happy to see you, Antonio," she said melodiously, watching carefully for the effect she had on him.

Clearly, she expected more. A brief preoccupied expression flickered across her face, but she rushed to replace it with a carefree demeanor.

"Have a seat. It has been so long since we'd seen each other. You look tanned and a bit thinner. A little haggard. Are you working a lot?" she asked and thought, *"Why is he so apathetic today? Not a single compliment, no sighing, no looking at me longingly. Have I lost my power over him?"*

"Yes, I am working a lot," Presto replied, settling onto a soft low poof.

"So I've heard. You are starting your own company. It is bound to be something original, like anything that comes from Antonio Presto."

Presto ignored the flattery and nodded.

"Yes, very original, Miss Lux."

"You must have come up with some wonderful new parts, haven't you?"

"Oh, yes. I think the part of the female lead came out great."

"How interesting. Please, do tell."

"You are acting as if you wouldn't mind participating in my project," Presto said with a barely noticeable smile.

Lux hesitated with the answer. This was exactly what she wanted – to let Presto know that she wouldn't mind working for him, if he really asked her, and if the screenplay and the role were to her liking, but at the same time, Lux wanted to avoid giving a definite answer that would tie her down.

"What actor doesn't dream of a winning role?" she replied.

She expected that Presto would start talking up the role of the female lead to make her more interested. But Antonio's answer was unexpected, "I am afraid this role is not for you," and added, "you won't be able to handle it."

This was a challenge, almost an insult.

"I might not like the role," she objected in an icy tone, "but not being able to handle it? You should know better, Antonio," she added more gently, with a friendly reproach.

"Yes, I know the kind of actress you are!"

"He didn't even say 'brilliant' or even 'talented'," Lux thought with vexation.

"A king's daughter, a countess, a young widow of a millionaire, a famous actress," Presto named some of Lux's best roles. "Stunning costumes, silk, gold, jewels, gorgeous hairdos... But that is nothing like what I have, Miss Lux."

"Then what do you have?" Lux said in an offended tone. "Who is your heroine?"

"A laundress."

"A laundress?" she barely whispered, staring at Antonio with wide eyes. Was he mocking her?

"Yes, an ordinary laundress, although a young and pretty one," Presto replied calmly. "And the hero... the hero is a jobless vagrant dressed in rags, who digs through trash bins and collects food scraps and other refuse. The setting is basements, garrets and back yards."

Lux somewhat regained her self-control and smiled.

"You are joking, Antonio."

"I am absolutely serious. Of course, I would have been very happy if my laundress had your appearance. The contrast between the wealth bestowed upon the heroine by nature and her position in life would have been very effective, but I think you would have trouble adopting such an image."

Lux's face suddenly lost all its charm. It became cold and almost evil. Gedda abandoned all interest in Presto. He was a doomed man in her eyes. Pitch didn't need to worry – Presto would break his own neck.

"Well then, what do you think of the new role, Miss?" he asked, barely hiding his irony.

"Look for your heroine among laundresses, Mister Presto," she replied coldly.

"That's exactly what I'll do," Presto said with daring playfulness and thought, *"Humble little Ellen is a pearl compared to this trash."*

There was nothing for them to talk about. Presto bowed and left.

Lux remained motionless on her Egyptian settee. She really did look like Cleopatra stung in the heart by a snake. Let Presto crash and burn – she didn't care. But how could he fall out of love with her so easily? Was she beginning to lose her feminine charm? This thought struck her cold. Her attraction was her capital. "No, no," she reassured herself, "not a single mirror is telling me that I am beginning to fade. It's something else. Maybe it's a consequence of the transformation Presto went through, or maybe he became involved with... some laundress. All the worse for him! And he dared to dream about me!"

While Presto was driving home, he was also thinking about Lux, "She is still one of the most beautiful women in the world. There is no question about that. But the more you come to know her as a person, the more you are disappointed. She has no purpose in life except for money and profit. No, these are not the right stars for my sky. A new business requires new people, and I shall find us among the talented young actors!"

On the steps of his villa Presto ran into Sebastian who looked somewhat embarrassed.

"We have guests," he said.

"Who?" Antonio asked carelessly, assuming someone came to discuss the business.

"The tenants. The elderly gentleman and the young lady." And Sebastian gave Presto a mischievous look.

"It's Barry!" Presto exclaimed. "Finally! Where are they?"

"Upstairs. They are unpacking and washing up after the trip. Missis Irwin is helping them."

Missis Irwin was a respectable widow who moved in several days ago to serve as Ellen's companion.

"Excellent! Excellent!" Antonio exclaimed energetically. "Have breakfast served in the blue sitting room. For four people!"

ELLEN BEGINS A NEW LIFE

"I am so happy to see you, my dear Barry," Presto said at breakfast. "I've been waiting for you most impatiently. We have tons of work to do."

"I was delayed by the management while they were looking for a suitable replacement. They are very selective and collect detailed information about every new employee – whether he is a union member, whether he participated in any strikes and other things like that."

"Things will get easier now," Presto said and started discussing the current business situation with Barry, occasionally glancing at Ellen and Missis Irwin.

The widow was a stout, phlegmatic woman with graying hair. She was entirely absorbed in her meal. More than anything she was fond of a good meal and a nap in an armchair. This new job was more than satisfactory. Nothing was required of her, aside from living in the house and staying out of the way. A pleasant service!

Ellen was enjoying her breakfast with the appetite of a young healthy person, but also carefully listened to the conversation and occasionally glanced at Presto. She was dressed in a simple dress of pale-colored canvas, carefully washed and ironed with her own hands.

After breakfast, Missis Irwin retired to her room adjacent to Ellen's – to take a nap to the chattering of her old friend, a green parrot, while Presto gave Barry and Ellen a tour of the villa.

He expected that Ellen, nature's child that she was, would feel awkward in the strange surroundings, but she didn't show a hint of discomfort. She was not dazzled by the uncommon beauty and luxury of the villa, although she expressed great interest toward the works of art collected by Presto. As he pointed at the paintings and sculptures, Presto named their authors, and Ellen often added to his explanations. Apparently, her uncle worked hard on her education.

The enormous library dressed in carved oak delighted Ellen.

"So many books!" she exclaimed.

The girl ran from one bookcase to the next with insatiable curiosity, from one row of stacks to another, deftly climbing up and down the ladders and pulling out one book after another. Barry was also very interested in the library. As if guided by intuition, he quickly found a vast biology section, examined the shelves with his trained eye, saw the beautiful editions of the Natural History classics, as well as the gorgeous illustrated reference books, and exclaimed, "I didn't expect that a movie actor would be so interested in scientific works!"

"Probably not just any actor, but a truly great actor," Ellen said from a ladder, unexpectedly to herself.

These sincere praises pleased Presto very much.

"Anyone who wants to do some serious work needs to learn a lot," he said. "The reference portion of this library alone has over five thousand volumes. There you will find the history of costumes of all eras and all people, works on architecture, and drawings of furniture and everyday objects."

"I could stay here forever!" Ellen exclaimed honestly.

"You can!" Presto replied, watching the girl's every move as she kept climbing up and down the stacks.

He pointed at a huge niche with floor-to-ceiling windows with northern exposure to keep the hot sunlight from interfering with work, and asked, "How do you like this little corner?"

The floor was carpeted. Round tables were decorated with lamps under silk shades and piled with the latest American and European magazines and newspapers. In a gap between the windows stood a bust of Athena surrounded by fresh flowers.

"Very much," Ellen replied.

"Well, if you would like, you can work here. I shall add you to the screenplay department."

"A depa-a-a-rtment?" Ellen said. "What will I do?"

"You will keep track of newspapers and magazines and cut out articles. I will show you what I am looking for. This is interesting work. And in your free time the entire library will be at your disposal. Agreed?"

"I will try if you think I can manage."

"You can!" Presto replied confidently.

However, he had no plans to keep the girl on this particular job. While he was still living by the Emerald Lake, he decided that Ellen should be an actress to play new roles in the new films. She had all the required abilities. He would work toward this goal carefully and unobtrusively. In the meantime, he had to give Ellen something to do to keep her from getting bored. Besides, she would enjoy earning her own living.

Presto knew how many obstacles were in his way. Antonio remembered the mistrust and prejudice with which Ellen treated his suggestion to try out as an actress. "I wouldn't know which way to turn!" she said. In the meantime, all he wanted from her was to remain herself in front of the camera. This too was a danger to his plans. He knew how quickly women became assimilated in the new surroundings, how well they could imitate others to fit into them. The simple dress she wore this morning calmed him down a little, but then he thought that having lived by the Emerald Lake, Ellen had no other choice. There were no fabrics, no good seamstress, no fashion magazines, and probably no money. What would happen to her when she entered the acting circles? Not a single woman, especially a young one, would want to look like Cinderella compared to others. Ellen would start dressing up, or worse, imitating the gestures, the manners, and whatever else was wrong with these artificial mannequins. There was nothing more terrible, tasteless, or vulgar than a fake, a failed imitation of aristocratic manners. Then Ellen would be lost for the big screen. Presto hoped that healthy simplicity instilled by her earlier life, and the sensible upbringing by her uncle Barry would keep her from the path of corruption.

Sebastian came into the library and said, "Sir, you are wanted at the office!"

Presto gave a heavy sigh. He did not want to leave, but he hadn't been to the office yet, and he knew there were dozens of people waiting for him there.

"Very well. Tell them I am leaving right away," he replied and turned to Barry. "Well, sir, if you are not too tired, come with me. I shall introduce you to my closest associates."

UNEXPECTED SUCCESS

The further things went, the more obstacles Presto had to overcome. He was faced with all the powers of American public opinion and money. The newspapers were filled with the dirtiest insinuations and gossip about the former favorite, who "had sold out to the commies." The campaign against "the man who lost his face" was revived anew. The press demanded another trial to take away Presto's property rights. In order to keep them at bay, Presto had to keep signing more high-dollar checks to the enterprising but greedy Piers. He was under a threat of criminal charges for stealing medications from Zorn and for "poisoning" the entire group of movie industry employees and public servants, such as the prosecutor and the governor.

For several days in a row, the papers published an interview with Lux – the woman certainly knew how to take her revenge!

She said that Presto "begged her on his knees to participate in his project and save him from certain disaster." But she refused his proposal indignantly, not wishing to be involved in this filthy, antisocial and criminal enterprise directed against American people and the honor of American democracy.

While he searched for pieces of interest in the newspapers, Ellen also read these articles. Whenever she met with Presto she expressed her utmost indignation. Presto regretted giving her this particular job, although he found Ellen's sincere outrage moving. There was something more in her anger than the sense of offended justice, and he watched the girl with renewed interest.

"It's alright, Miss Ellen! This was to be expected, and there are no surprises here for me. Struggle to the death is one of the fundamental principles of our glorious democracy. And struggle we shall. Will you help me?"

"I am ready to do anything I can to help you!" Ellen exclaimed warmly and sincerely.

Presto was touched. He took her hand and said, "Perhaps, I will need your assistance very soon. Don't forget your promise!"

He decided to take advantage of her mood and get her to agree to be in the film. Presto was having trouble with his heroine, the laundress. The well-known experienced actresses refused to play a laundress, and the young ones, who were under the influence of movie star conditioning, could not handle the role. Their laundresses resembled night club dancers or countesses trying to do laundry, but were far from the image of a real female worker. That is why the rehearsals continued without any filming.

To distract Ellen from the upsetting newspapers and achieve his goal quicker, Presto frequently said to her, "Enough about the press. Won't you come to the studio with me?"

The girl happily agreed. She was very interested in the mysterious, behind-the-scenes side of cinema. Presto cleverly developed his strategy. In her presence, he purposely tried out the least suitable actresses for the lead female role. When they minced around the washtub as if they were dancing foxtrot, or pulled the clothes out with two fingers and a raised pinky, like a chocolate from a box, Ellen couldn't help but smile and make mocking remarks, and sometimes exclaimed in astonishment, "How silly! Doesn't she know how it's done? Hasn't she ever seen how clothes are washed, rinsed, and hung up to dry?"

"Why don't you show her?" Presto once said with an innocent face. Ellen was taken aback but he continued, "You will simply do her a great favor. I hope you are not ashamed of being able to do laundry?"

Presto had hit the target.

"Not at all," she replied. "I don't think any manual work is demeaning. Allow me!" Ellen addressed the actress, and got to work with the same artlessness, as if she was still at the cabin on the shore of the Emerald Lake.

Fortunately, Presto's concerns were in vain – Ellen lost none of the simplicity and naturalness of her movements. Antonio held his breath as he watched her work, and Hoffman, who was at his post by the camera even though there was no filming, grunted and suddenly cranked up the camera.

"Even Hoffman couldn't resist!" Presto thought happily.

The actors watched Ellen carefully and with some surprise. The studio became completely quiet. The silence was broken only by the dry crackling of the camera. Ellen kept doing laundry as if nothing was amiss. When she finally finished, Hoffman stopped the camera and roared, "We got it! We got it, damn it! It came out damnably well!"

The actors, mostly young and unaffected by the spirit of jealousy, started applauding. Without realizing it, Ellen showed them all the epitome of any art – simplicity.

Only now, when she saw the unexpected effect of her performance, did she feel awkward and blush. Everyone was congratulating her, Hoffman was beside himself. He was shaking both of Ellen's hands and shouting, "We are going to win! You are a born…"

"Laundress!" Ellen said.

"A born actress! Believe me, the old wolf! You already have what others get through work and years of study."

"It's probably because actors act," Ellen objected, "and I wasn't even thinking about it."

"You lived. That's exactly what we need," Hoffman insisted. "The more acting and artifice, the worse. You've heard many times, when Mister Presto asked the actors, 'Please, don't act!'"

And so Ellen was voted in as an actress by those who saw her first performance, even before she agreed to it.

But she still didn't believe it and had doubts.

When she and Presto were returning home in his car, she remained quiet for a long time. Presto kept glancing at her out of the corner of his eyes, and also kept mum. Let her get over the initial anxiety. Only when they were halfway there, did he ask, "Well?"

"I still don't want to be an actress," she replied.

"Why?"

"Your conclusion is too hasty," she replied. "What did I do? I worked like I normally would. Anyone can do that, if he is given his usual work to do. A carpenter would have whittled, a digger would have dug, and of course, they would have done a better job than an actor who had only just picked up a jointer or a spade. But your heroine in the movie doesn't just do laundry. She is happy, she suffers, she cries, she laughs, she talks, she thinks, and that is not the same thing as washing clothes. No, I will not act. I will disgrace myself and ruin the movie."

"You are right to a point," Presto said, "but only to a point. Of course, we would have to do a lot of work. But the same is the case with actors who pick up a jointer or a spade for the first time, because we have to make sure that the real carpenters and diggers don't make fun of them when they see them on screen. The most important thing is that you have a natural talent and unquestionable ability. I saw it back at the Emerald Lake when you portrayed Ophelia's madness. Trust my experience and Hoffman's experience. He's dealt with hundreds of novices before and can evaluate a person from a single movement or a single gesture."

Ellen refused to give up and objected, "But I was just moving as I was used to."

"Understand," Presto continued trying to convince her, "it's one thing to do laundry at the park ranger's cabin, and a different thing to do the same before the camera. Even the best laundress might forget her normal routine when she knows she is being filmed. She either feels awkward and can't do her work, or she starts working the way she thinks is necessary for the screen. Only truly talented people can withstand the trial by filming."

At the back of his mind, Presto himself was not entirely certain of this, but Ellen was undoubtedly the best raw material with the greatest promise compared to the others. Ellen did not know that Presto asked Hoffman in advance to support him, and encourage Ellen if he too discovered that she was a good fit. Ellen must have had a serious effect on Hoffman, judging by the sincere emotion with which he greeted her debut. As for the other actors, they were delighted not only by the naturalness but also by the beauty and the harmony of her movements. What Presto noticed back by the Emerald Lake was a revelation even to some of the more experienced actors – that working movements can be as beautiful and graceful as carefully choreographed routines, that even the cleverest devices could not show off the beauty of form, the line, the dynamic of a living human body as well as these simple poses and gestures.

Noticing Ellen's continued hesitation, Presto said, "Listen, Miss Ellen, just recently you told me you would do anything to help me. You can help me now. You know I am going through difficult times. Everything is hanging by a thread. In the case of failure, I will go bankrupt and my career will be over. In my downfall, I am bound to draw others with me – everyone who threw their lot in with me. After all, when I started this project, I wasn't just thinking about myself. I told you that back at the park. Don't refuse, Ellen. Please, understand that Hoffman and I would never let you fail. We are as interested in success as you are, and we shall do everything possible to make this success possible. Just give me your agreement!"

"If that is the case, I agree," Ellen finally said.

Presto let out a sigh of relief and exclaimed, "There you go!" He smiled and said, "Now your fate is tied with mine too. We shall either win together or lose together!"

PRESTO'S NEW FACE DEVELOPS

This was a great victory and the first great joy Presto experienced since he started this unequal struggle.

Work at the studio acquired a new interest to him. Presto was an extremely strict and demanding director. To save film, he didn't shoot the same scene dozens of time, as it was commonly done in Hollywood. Only after endless rehearsals, when he was completely satisfied with the acting, Hoffman was allowed to film, and there were hardly any scenes that had to be shot twice. Presto brought one troublesome young actress almost to tears before he finally got what he wanted. He himself transformed into every role to show them how to act. He became agitated and angry, sometimes even shouted at the actors or collapsed on the couch in desperation and exhaustion, only to resume the drill a few minutes later. Fortunately, he no longer had to deal with laughter he had inevitably inspired in the past, when he was a freak. The actors patiently tolerated everything. They saw the usefulness of this difficult schooling and developed before his very eyes.

Presto made no exceptions for Ellen. He was as stern with her as he was with others. To his joy, he was not mistaken in his expectations. Ellen was extremely capable. It became clear that she would handle the role of the heroine beautifully.

When it came to filming, and the actors were in costume and makeup, Presto showed up as well, also fully dressed, but completely unrecognizable – he was good-natured and happy, as if he didn't show up for work but for a game of polo. This improved everyone's mood. There was no more strict, pedantic teacher, but a merry playmate, and the game began.

As he ran the camera, Hoffman didn't watch a single actor with the same attention as he watched Presto in his new image and his new role.

Hoffman's first impressions were undefined. The new face developed slowly, as if on a film with a weak developing solution. Presto's image didn't have the characteristic features of a familiar mask, with which the spectators recognized their favorite comedians. He was not a man in a mask, but rather a man from the masses. His face resembled thousands of other faces, his threadbare clothes were no different from those of thousands of other unemployed. Antonio was no longer a toy freak, a marionette, who passively accepted the blows of fate, fell, rose, and fell again, inspiring no pity but only laughter, as if he were an inanimate object.

The new Presto also received some strikes from the fates and he also ended up in various unpleasant and awkward situations. But not only did he rise every time, but he invariably plunged into battle against his oppressors, no matter how much stronger they were. This provoked laughter but also genuine human sympathy. The new Presto's acting touched deeper human emotions. Injustices, beatings, and insults Presto sustained evoked laughter, immediately followed by indignation, protest, and the desire to help.

The more they filmed, the more Hoffman was surprised and astonished. Along with the physical transformation, Presto underwent a wonderful intellectual metamorphosis. The new Presto inherited from the old one all of his humorous power, despite the fact that his new physical appearance had no comical disfigurement. The new Presto possessed another precious quality, which the old Presto may have also had, but it never reached the audience because it was obscured by his physical ugliness – deep humanity.

Once, during a break, Hoffman walked up to Presto, firmly shook his hand and said, "You surpassed all my expectations, Antonio. I no longer doubt that you have found your new face. And with a face like that we cannot help but win."

Presto smiled happily, but his voice was sad, "In the meantime, I have never been as far from victory as I am right now. Come see me in the evening, Hoffman. There is much I need to talk to you about."

FAITHFUL FRIEND TO THE END

The same evening Hoffman came into Presto's study.

"The film is nearing the end, but my savings are nearing the end even faster. I am bankrupt, Hoffman, and we won't be able to finish the picture," Presto said glumly.

Hoffman frowned and remained silent.

"Money is flowing away like water," Presto continued. "Every week I am signing checks for several million dollars. I only have enough money left for two weeks, but even for that I had to mortgage my villa with all its furnishings. I am no longer the master in my own house."

"This was to be expected," Hoffman said.

"Yes, I made a mistake in calculations," Presto said with a nod. "Not in the expenses to produce the movie. It's costing even less than I expected. We are saving on film and on outdoor shots, we are managing almost entirely without sets and saving on light, on extras, and on costumes that cost us pennies. I have no screenplay department with dozens of writers, playwrights and literary experts. You know I stayed up nights writing the script, after the insane amount of work during the day. I worked like a madman, without sleep, saving wherever I could. If it was only about the production, we would have had money left over. But, I admit, I underestimated the resistance and, more importantly, the cunning of our enemies. You know the kind of underhanded trickery they used to destroy me – the battle took place before your eyes. Wherever we went, we felt the powerful hand of large corporations and banks subsidizing and monopolizing the movie industry. The suppliers refused to sell us the equipment and even the film. We had to use third parties and pay three times as much for everything. The movie distributors and cinema owners told us in advance that they would not allow my film on the big screen. And so we had to build our own move theater. Each one of them cost a million, except for the one near San Francisco, where we used your idea."

Hoffman nodded. At some point he gave Presto an idea to lease a section of an old military airfield near San Francisco and built a movie theater there, or rather, just a projection booth and a giant screen to be able to play movies not only in the evenings, but also in full daylight. There was no theater, per se, in this open-air cinema, no rows of chairs. The spectators could drive into the airfield in their cars and watch the movie without having to step out.

"This novelty," Presto continued, "should attract the public and serve as good publicity. But it won't save us. Besides, such cinema is only accessible to those who own cars, and you know that my bet is on the lower-class working people. And so I had to build large enclosed cinemas in the biggest American cities."

Hoffman knew all this, and Presto was only telling him about his difficulties because he was summarizing and verifying where he made mistakes.

"After all is said and done, the balance is zero, and the work is not finished," he concluded dismally and looked questioningly at Hoffman, waiting for his answer.

"I thought as much," Hoffman said. "What can we do? The banks won't help us, there is no sense to even think about it. And we won't find a sufficiently careless private lender who could give us the money, even with the loan shark interest rate, to support a bankrupt and clearly hopeless enterprise. Which means, if we want to continue the struggle, we must find internal resources. Of course, I have some personal savings, but I doubt they will help the situation."

"I wouldn't take a single penny of your savings, Hoffman, even if it could help the situation," Presto objected. "It's bad enough that you committed to working in such an odious enterprise."

Hoffman barely concealed his joy and rushed to explain his position, "You are right, my friend, more right than you think. I have jeopardized my career by participating in your project."

"And if it goes bust, then most likely you won't be hired anywhere else, and then you will need your savings more than ever," Presto came to his aid, noticing him fidgeting in his chair.

"Yes, yes," Hoffman wanted to finish this unpleasant conversation. "And I might need them sooner than I'd like."

"Indeed? What are you trying to say?"

Hoffman spread his hands, sighed, and replied, "The thing is…I've been hinted… even got a kind of ultimatum…"

"To leave me?" Presto understood.

"Yes, to sever all ties with you. If I don't, then all producers intend to boycott me, and my career in the movie industry will be over."

"What have you decided?"

"Why are you looking at me like Caesar at Brutus, Presto?" Hoffman asked in embarrassment.

"I am waiting for the last stab, my Brutus," Presto replied coldly.

"I haven't decided anything yet, my Caesar," Hoffman defended himself just as coldly. "I only considered it necessary to warn you." The awkwardness of the situation suddenly made him angry and he exclaimed abruptly, "What can I do? One man cannot resist an army."

"I am not asking anything of you, Hoffman," Presto said sadly. "Don't get so upset. It's all understandable and normal."

A pregnant pause followed.

"Damn life!" Hoffman grumbled. "Believe me, if it was in my power to help you…"

"You would have helped, and there is no need to talk about it anymore. You are free to do as you wish, and I… I might figure something out," Presto said and held out his hand. Hoffman shook it and left, stepping heavily.

Presto stood there for a long time, looking down. He then whispered with a bitter smile, "A faithful friend to the end. What now? Only a good wizard can help me now. Unfortunately, it doesn't happen in real life."

ORANGE BLOSSOMS

Presto woke up at six in the morning in his large white bedroom, where windows remained closed, and purified, cool air was supplied by the air conditioning system. Glancing around the room, Presto thought, *"Soon, I will have to part with all this."* Then he sighed and looked at the clock. "I could stay in bed another fifteen minutes," and he reached out to the nightstand with the stack of the last evening's papers. He was so tired the night before that he didn't read them.

He opened the first newspaper and scanned through it. One article attracted his attention. Presto started reading it and frowned more and more. He then balled up the paper, threw it on the floor and exclaimed indignantly, "This is revolting!" He leaned back on the pillows and seemingly froze. He remained motionless, with his face stony, for some time. Only his drawn eyebrows and fast breathing betrayed his agitation and frantic work taking place in his brain. Twenty minutes passed, and he remained in the same pose.

Suddenly, like a man who solved a difficult problem, he came back to life and abruptly pressed an electric call button.

"Sebastian! Hot water for shaving, quickly! Prepare my suit!" he said to his old servant, while he himself, still in his pajamas and slippers, rushed to the bathroom decorated with pink marble.

"Do you know if Miss Ellen is up?" he asked through the open door, when Sebastian brought hot water.

"The young lady always rises with birds," the old man replied.

"Still faithful to her old habits," Antonio thought with a smile and said, "Excellent! Have coffee served on the verandah and tell Geoffrey to prepare the car."

In a few minutes he ran up to the second floor, quickly walked down the long corridor and slowed down next to Ellen's door. He stood next to it, listening to the girl's singing from within, caught his breath, got rid of the last traces of preoccupation on his face, and knocked.

Ellen opened the door. The rays of morning sun gilded her hair and her white dress.

"Mister Presto!" she exclaimed with surprise but no displeasure. "What is the meaning of this early visit?"

"Miss Ellen!" Presto replied merrily. "It's a beautiful morning and it occurred to me that we could go for a ride before heading to the studio. We have a lot of work to do today, some of the most difficult scenes, and nothing is ever as refreshing as the morning air."

Presto's carefree, happy mood was infectious. It's been a long time since she'd seen him so happy.

"Excellent thought!" the girl replied with a smile.

"Then let's go, come on! Coffee is ready, and while we have breakfast, the driver will fuel the car and pull up."

Scorching themselves with coffee and joking around, they were acting like two school kids who came up with an amusing prank and were in a hurry to carry it out.

A short low beep sounded from the entrance, announcing that the car was ready.

"Do you hear that?" Presto said. "Our destiny is calling upon us. Let us be off to meet it!"

Presto's words and behavior that morning were very mysterious.

Soon, the last of Hollywood's buildings remained behind them. The smooth road stretched into the distance. Dark blue mountains loomed on the horizon. The clear California sky gazed down upon the fertile land. The morning air was still fresh and filled with the bitter scent of grasses. Presto and Ellen breathed deeply.

"How lovely!" Ellen exclaimed and squinted at the still-low sun.

"Yes, we haven't seen any nature in a long time," Presto replied.

His face and pose reflected deep satisfaction, like a person who had just survived a difficult operation.

"Remember our cabin by the Emerald Lake?" he continued dreamily.

Laughing and arguing, they started remembering various incidents.

"You were a very strict landlady," Presto joked. "You were ruthless when you had to clean the room and kicked Pip and me out."

"There is no other way to handle men," Ellen replied. "They don't understand that they are in the way."

"With men?" Presto laughed. "Incidentally, what was the fate of the other man subject to this abuse?"

Ellen gave Presto a questioning glance.

"You used to put me outside along with Pip. What happened to him?"

"He is in good hands," Ellen replied and added with a sigh. "I wasn't sure whether it was alright to move into your house with the dog."

"We will have him shipped over!" Presto exclaimed, noticing a note of sadness in Ellen's tone.

Low white stone farm fences started appearing by the sides of the road. Orange trees were in full bloom. Clusters of white flowers stood out against dark greenery like snow. Delicate fragrance filled the air.

"Look at all these orange blossoms for future brides!" Presto exclaimed.

In one spot, the branches hung over the fence all the way to the pavement.

"Stop, Geoffrey!" Presto told the driver.

The car halted. Presto jumped out, picked a few branches and came back.

"Go ahead."

The car moved on. Presto handed the orange blossoms to Ellen.

"Pin this to your dress. And this one to your hair. There you go. One bride is ready."

Ellen blushed, pulled a small mirror from her purse and looked at herself. In a white dress, with white orange blossoms she truly looked like a bride.

"All you need is a veil!" Presto noted, admiring Ellen.

"What a matchmaker!" Ellen said with a frown. "Who are you marrying me off to?"

Presto looked her in the eyes, paused, looked down and replied quietly and seriously, "To myself."

Ellen grew pale and lowered her eyes.

"Your jokes are going too far, sir," she said sternly.

"I am not joking," Presto continued just as seriously. "Miss Ellen! Remember what I told you when you agreed to play the female lead? 'Your fate is now tied to my fate.' Why not make these ties even stronger? I couldn't wish for a better wife."

This was so unexpected that Ellen leaned back in her seat and seemed to be in a swoon. Her eyes were closed, her face grew even paler. Then her lips shook and she whispered, still looking down, "I cannot be your wife, Mister Presto!"

"Why?"

"Because… Because you are a famous actor, a millionaire, and I am an ordinary poor girl. Even poor girls have their pride, sir."

"I am a famous actor? I am a millionaire?" Presto exclaimed, then lowered his voice and continued. "Yes, I was a famous actor in my previous guise. But now I am a beginner, an unknown young actor, just like you. Yes, I was a millionaire. But presently, I am as poor as you are. Did you know that even the villa we are living in has been mortgaged and we might all get kicked out if I don't pay the debt on time? As you can see, we are equals. In fact, you are better off than I am. Because a girl like you can always find a better match."

"I have never viewed marriage as a profitable deal," she objected heatedly. "I am not afraid of poverty and hardship."

"Then what is the matter? You don't like me? You don't love me?"

"You love someone else," Ellen avoided giving the direct answer.

"Do you mean Miss Lux?" Presto asked. "Yes, I used to be drawn by her beauty. But when I came to know her better as a person, I became convinced that she and I were completely different people. During my last business meeting with her, I myself was struck by how little I was affected by her charm. Even then I realized the reason for this – I met you."

Color was returning to Ellen's cheeks.

"Why do you propose at this specific time? It's so sudden and so badly timed, considering…"

"Yes, this may seem badly timed. But moments such as this are the best to test one's sincerity and strength. You know the tragedy of people who are wealthy and famous. This tragedy is never being certain, whether they win someone's heart and hand out of love, or whether it's because of their fame and money. The only true love comes from someone who will not turn away from their beloved during the difficult times, in the face of poverty and brutal struggle, as my movie shows. Be your heroine not only on screen but in life! It would give me new strength," he concluded sincerely and carefully put his hand over Ellen's, anxiously waiting for her answer.

She took a deep breath, paused and finally replied, "In happiness or in grief, I shall not leave you, Presto. That is, if you love me."

"And you? Do you love me?"

"I fell in love with you back by the Emerald Lake. Before I knew that you were Antonio Presto."

Presto kissed her hand and shouted, "Geoffrey! To the studio! At full speed! I think we might already be running late."

EXTRAS DOWNSTAGE

"First, let's stop by the office to see your uncle," Presto said.

Barry was very surprised when he saw Presto enter his office, along with Ellen wearing orange blossoms.

"Mister Barry!" Antonio exclaimed after saying hello to the old man. "I came to announce our engagement. I hope, as Miss Ellen's guardian and next of kin, you have nothing against our marriage?"

Barry wanted to say something, but his breath caught from anxiety. He coughed, then said, "Congratulations. I am very glad. But this is very unexpected!"

"For parents and guardians, it often is," Presto replied with a laugh and firmly shook the old teacher's hand. "And now," he continued, "I have something to ask you. Right now, immediately, send an announcement of the upcoming nuptials to all the newspapers."

"What for?" Ellen wondered.

"This is how it's done," Presto replied. "And now, Miss Ellen, let us off to the studio."

When they entered the set, Presto noticed that something unusual was happening. The place was full – the entire staff, workers, set designers, and actors were present. This included those who were not involved in scenes being filmed that day. The set pieces had been moved aside. The only thing remaining was a lectern, from which the director normally provided his instructions. Everyone's mood was elevated. Their faces were lively and moved. It was as if everyone was waiting for something.

One of the extras stepped out from the crowd and said loudly, "The entire team is aware of the challenges facing our enterprise. Workers, staff and actors are all concerned about it. Unfortunately, Mister Presto hasn't discussed the situation with the rest of us. We would like for him to do so today."

Antonio Presto could not help but acknowledge the validity of this reproach. Accustomed to working independently, he acted not like the leader of a cooperative enterprise, but like a director of a commercial firm. He thought that as long as his collaborators were promised their share of the dividends, nothing else was required. Presto openly recognized his mistake, blaming it on his lack of experience in communal matters.

Then the extras' representative said that the following decision had been made during a meeting of the entire company: everyone agreed to receive half of their salary, or even less, if necessary, until the picture was finished.

This was a great relief for Presto and he started thanking them, but there were exclamations from the crowd, "It's alright! It's our shared project! Shared interest! We'd rather have half a salary than be unemployed!"

"Wrong again!" Presto thought, annoyed with himself.

A quick meeting followed, during which a committee was elected to help manage the company. The committee members chose Presto as their chairman.

Presto's enterprise was getting off to a new start and changing its structure.

Hoffman frowned and stayed away. He was offered to join the audit commission but refused.

When business matters were taken care off, the workers returned to their works with the enthusiasm of soldiers preparing to storm an enemy fortress.

While the set was being straightened out following the meeting, Hoffman pulled Presto off to the side, his expression troubled, and said, "I wanted to warn you about a new problem pertaining to you personally and…"

"Are you talking about the new campaign started by the evening papers?"

"I am also talking about today's morning papers. They have stooped to a new level of shamelessness."

"Ah, that's right, I forgot to tell my teammates some news!" Presto exclaimed, seemingly forgetting about the papers, and walked toward Ellen.

Hoffman was confused. He thought it strange that Presto paid so little attention to the new press campaign and ran off to announce some kind of news instead of discussing it.

Presto walked up to Ellen, took her hand and said loudly, "Hello! Please pause for a minute!"

The studio became expectantly quiet.

"I forgot, my dear friends, to share my happiness with you. Miss Ellen Kay did me the honor by agreeing to become my wife."

Ellen was taken aback and thought, "Why is he making our engagement so public? It's as if he is in a hurry to make sure everyone knows."

There were congratulations and even applause. Everyone ran to Presto and Ellen. Presto's hand hurt from being shaken so many times – he felt like the president during a reception at the White House.

Actresses who were intrigued by Ellen's orange blossoms from the start surrounded her in a dense circle. Ellen was observant and noticed that some of them looked at her with seeming pity, some were hiding a chuckle, and some smiled with insulting duplicity.

"Why are they looking at me like that?" she thought, feeling awkward and worried. "Perhaps, they are just jealous," Ellen consoled herself.

The set was back in place, and filming began. The actors had never played with such energy. Presto and Ellen surpassed themselves.

Hoffman ran the camera and was uncommonly moved. If the movie continued at this level to the end, it was bound to become a world-renowned masterpiece, and Hoffman would get his share of the glory. Everyone loved the victor.

"Enough!" Presto shouted when the chattering of the camera stopped. "We have done some great work today. We didn't have to re-do a single scene."

AN UNEXPECTED SETBACK

Having returned from the studio, Ellen went to her room. She was tired after all the work and other tribulations of the day. She wanted to sort out what happened. Ellen carefully put the orange blossom clusters into a vase, touched the fragrant white flowers with her lips, and settled into a deep armchair.

Wasn't life incredible? Like a fanciful movie with sudden twists and turns in the plot, as Presto would say it. First there were the soothing views of the Emerald Lake. The silence broken only by the distant noise of the geysers, their repeating, monotonous rhythm marking days, weeks, and months – all of them similar to one another.

Suddenly, it was as if a mad projectionist accelerated the projector to a mad speed.

The trip, the stations, the cities, new impressions, new people... Presto's villa... And there she was – plain little Ellen Kay – a movie actress, with Antonio Presto as her fiancé.

She was happy and a little scared. Other actresses looked at her so strangely back at the studio. Were they really so envious? Well, let them! Ellen was filled with pride. She triumphed over all these overdressed mannequins! It was a pity that Antonio had so many problems and disappointments. Why were people so mean? What did Antonio ever do to them?

But this would pass. Everything would settle down. And she would be happy with Antonio. They would have children. Life would not be complete without children. If they had a boy, she would call him Antonio, and if a girl, then...

Ellen turned her head as if looking for an answer, and saw several letters on a side table by the armchair.

She was surprised. She had never received any letters until then, but now, there were several. Were they engagement cards? But they couldn't have come so quickly.

Ellen opened the first envelope. It contained a folded newspaper article. Ellen started reading it and suddenly felt as if she was running out of air.

The article was about Presto and herself.

"The once-famous movie actor," the article said, "who made his career not as much with his questionable talent as with his exceptional disfigurement, has never been known for his morality. The newspaper has the most accurate testimony about filthy orgies this disgusting freak held at his villa. His moral ugliness had surpassed his limitless physical ugliness even then."

The description of the story with Miss Lux followed, in which "the cunning swindler without honor or conscience" made a move for her millions.

"Only Miss Lux's exceptional kindness spared him from life in prison," the article said, "or, perhaps, the electric chair this amoral person, this depraved monster fully deserves…

"His ugly dwarfish body was no longer enough to accommodate his crimes. Suspicious 'scientists' using illegal methods of treatment turned the little freak into a big scoundrel. His criminal 'creations' grew proportionately. The new Presto was no longer satisfied with secret crimes. Depraved to the core, he openly challenged morality and public opinion, mocking our good American mores. He walked all over them, insulted our most sacred feelings, and brought shame upon our country.

"He found a girl somewhere – may her name be known to all: one Ellen Kay, who is most likely as depraved as himself, or a fool unable to tell her right hand from her left when it comes to questions of morality. The illegitimate daughter of a park ranger from Yellowstone Park must have fallen for Antonio Presto's mythical millions. The photographs below – those of Ellen Kay by the window, with a mop in her hand, and Presto next to the same house – leave no doubt about the truthfulness of this story. Presto openly put her up at his house. He…"

Ellen could not read any further. Her reaction was more violent and acute than Antonio's. Ellen jumped out of her seat as if swept by a storm, and burst into Presto's study without knocking.

THE FATE OF THE FILM IS DECIDED

Presto took one look at Ellen and realized that she knew everything. He expected this. She would have found out sooner or later.

"Our engagement is off, and I am leaving your house immediately!" she exclaimed, looking at him angrily.

Presto rose but remained silent. He knew that he had to let this outburst of indignation flow freely.

"You deceived me! It wasn't love that made you propose to me. You were guided by the most noble, most chivalrous feelings. I understand that and I appreciate it. But I cannot accept this sacrifice. You felt sorry for me, and I… I believed that you loved me…"

The girls voice was halting, she was barely standing. She almost fell into an armchair, covered her face and burst into tears, like a deeply and undeservedly mistreated child.

Presto watched her with great sadness but kept quiet. She wanted her to get some relief in her tears. Only when her sobs subsided did he hand her a glass of water.

"Drink this and calm down," he said gently but also firmly, as if talking to the child she essentially was at the moment.

Her teeth chattered against the glass, water spilled onto the carpet, but she managed to drink a few sips and calm down. Presto said, "You have deeply offended me, Miss Ellen!"

Antonio reached his goal – she expected him to justify and defend himself, but he turned the tables on her and accused her. This surprise forced her to focus. Now she was capable of listening and understanding what she heard.

"I? Offended you?" the girl asked in confusion and stopped crying, only sniffing from time to time.

"Yes, you have deeply offended me," Presto repeated.

He pulled out blue silk handkerchief with white polka dots from his pocket and wiped her up. She was so struck by this liberty that she didn't know how to respond. Presto continued, "Let us not cry anymore. Nothing can be fixed with tears. You have offended me by doubting that I love you. I am not the terrible criminal the newspapers portray, but also not a knight in shining armor you imagined me to be. I am very sensitive to any injustice, but believe me, I wouldn't have rushed to propose to a girl simply because she was insulted, even if I was partially responsible for the insult. I admit, had it not been for these revolting newspaper article, I would not have proposed to you today, but tomorrow, or the day after. But I would have done it. The newspapers merely gave me a push, forced me to realize deeper and more acutely, how much I loved you, and how precious your interests and your honor were to me. Understand, even if you leave my house now, it would change nothing. Your reputation would already be stained. As someone who loves you, can I allow this to happen? Your departure would only fuel the gossip, give more fodder for the dirty slander and a strong proof that my enemies are right, and I am guilty. No, the only way to respond to the strike of these dishonorable and dishonest people, who didn't spare even you, who didn't pause before meddling in your private life and insulting your honor – is to respond with the blow of our own. Our marriage is bound to knock the weapons from their hands, shut them up and stop this campaign of defamation. That is why I rushed not only with my proposal but also with making it so public, which you were so surprised by. All shall become clear," he said after catching his breath, "if you think about the reasons that drove this despicable newspaper campaign. This is only one link in the chain of their struggle against me. They are doing their best to bring down my enterprise. They are not just afraid of competition. They are frightened that this might be the first step in uniting cinema workers against the moneybags. They are also frightened of my new artistic face they already know about – the one that uncovers the social ills of our country. That is why they are so obsessed with me. First they wanted to annihilate me by driving me to bankruptcy before my first picture came out. They almost succeeded, but I found support in my teammates. At the same time, my enemies constantly slandered my name. And now they decided to deal another underhanded blow – to use their lies to separate us, to drive us apart, to crush us emotionally, to cause a psychological trauma and, thus, disable the two lead actors in the film – you and me. They are hoping that the film will not be finished, even if I have enough money. The worse you react to their assault, the quicker they reach their goal and triumph. Are we really going to give them this satisfaction? Of course, getting through this is not going to be easy. I myself feel as if I aged twenty years in a few hours. But I am holding on and I think I acted better than ever today, even though I already knew of the newspaper articles since yesterday and was carrying this load in my head. One more thing. Not only you and I depend on the completion of this film, but also our team mates, who are prepared to surrender their wages to save the project.

Community organizations are also coming to our aid. Are we going to be weak and surrender? Will you leave me now and take back your word? The fate of the movie, the fate of the entire company is in your hands."

Ellen was no longer crying. But her face was filled with suffering. She hesitated. Presto watched her anxiously, waiting for an answer. Finally, she said, "It's very difficult, but I shall try to finish the picture."

"And be my wife?" Presto asked quickly.

"This question is even harder to answer right now. Don't rush me, Presto. Let me think."

"Very well. I shall wait. The work will calm you down and then we can take care about our personal matters. Isn't it so?"

Reassured and certain that all would be well, he kissed her hand.

TRIUMPH

The announcement of the upcoming marriage between Miss Ellen Kay and Mister Antonio Presto did its job. The newspaper campaign of slander and insinuation subsided. But there were traces of it left. Presto saw that Ellen was suffering deeply. As she played the role of the heroine, she gathered all her strength in order to focus, but her attention was clearly elsewhere. Some of the scenes had to be re-filmed, which hadn't happened since the filming began. Fortunately, the end of the script was full of tragic emotions for the hero and the heroine. Presto and Ellen could supplement their acting with their own feelings. Some of the scenes were filled with a strikingly powerful sense of reality. Even Hoffman, who was used to everything, felt unusual agitation and nervous tremor in his hands, as he held the camera. Ellen's acting sometimes rose to the level of pure genius. After the filming of such scenes ended, the studio remained uncommonly quiet. Everyone was struck and overwhelmed by the performance. Women and even some men had tears in their eyes. One time, a huge red-haired Scottish carpenter, who has been through a lot in his own life, suddenly gave a loud sniff and proceeded to cry, large teardrops rolling down his pale freckled face. He was surprised and taken aback by this. Never in his life had he cried over his own troubles, and here he broke down over a movie scene. But weren't there millions of similar people who had been through the same thing? Hoffman no longer had any doubts that this would be one of those world-famous classics that had the ability move hearts and bring forth tears. *"Perhaps, Presto was right in choosing this new path,"* Hoffman thought.

In the meantime, having finished the filming for the day, Presto became absorbed in business matters. He now had the committee to help him as well as the management of the now-official cooperative society. What he started was supported by others. This made him feel awkward at times, sometimes even angered him, because he was no longer the sole ruler in charge of the fate of the enterprise. It was difficult for him to get used to the new situation, but it was too late to back out – there was no other choice.

Soon it turned out that the team's giving up some of their wages was not entirely effective. They were still short on money. The committee and the management appealed to the unions and various grassroots organizations. Much to Hoffman's chagrin, the enterprise was taking on broader, increasingly more public character, becoming more "left" and more "commie". The struggle continued. The newspapers wrote about the financial disaster that was Presto's company, then that it was taken over by Jewish Masons, liberals, and communists, that Presto had "sold out to the commies" and became a toy in their hands. The most outrageous falsehoods were published about the film itself. The newspapers assured the readers that it struck at every foundation of politics and morality, civilization and religion, and all but threatened the very existence of the United States. Votes were being collected to prohibit the movie entirely.

In addition to all these troubles, Ellen clearly avoided Presto. They saw each other only at the studio. Using various excuses, Ellen refused to go home with Presto in the same car, and, once there, immediately locked herself in her room.

The work had to be done and the film had to be completed in these conditions. Still, it was completed.

It finally opened at Presto's cinemas and its success surpassed all expectations. People arrived in droves to see the film. The new Presto's acting evoked as much if not more laughter than Presto the freak. But there was something new in this laughter. It was no longer the animalistic, physiological laughter. Rather, it was laughter through tears.

The audiences were most impressed by the scenes that involved the unknown new actress Ellen Kay. The spectators crowding the movie theaters sensed the unusual simplicity and sincerity in Ellen's acting. The public was beside itself. One elderly woman with large red hands watched Ellen do laundry on screen and exclaimed loudly, "You can see this girl knows what she's doing! Where did they get her? Look at her go!"

To her, this was the ultimate praise.

Genuine art is understandable to all. The opinion of the old working woman coincided with those of several prominent movie critics who showed up to see the new film.

"Astonishing!" one of them said to his colleague. "Where did Presto find this actress? Believe me, she will overshadow the brightest stars of cinematography."

Presto, Ellen, and Hoffman sat in a separate box, watching carefully the effect of the film on the spectators. When the audience shook with laughter, or women were heard sobbing, touched by Ellen's acting, they couldn't help but glance at the screen.

"You see?" Presto said to Ellen. "And you were afraid that you might ruin the picture."

Hoffman smoked one cigar after another and grunted approvingly.

The incredible success did its job. Profit was profit, and "money didn't smell" no matter where it came from. Such was the attitude of the ancient Roman entrepreneurs who introduced this proverb. Many distributors could not resist the revenues brought in by the new film and started taking it into circulation. The beachhead was established. Individual managers were followed by companies, who, in turn, were followed by large corporations. The film began its triumphant march across America and Europe.

Even the publications from the enemy camp could not help but acknowledge the virtues of the script, the music, incidentally, written by Presto himself, and the acting. The new Presto and Ellen rose into the skies of world cinematography like two bright stars. The supporting cast and extras, nearly all of them young and obscure, also received credit for their astonishing acting, which placed Presto's talent as the director beyond doubt.

Pitch screamed and yelled in helpless rage.

"I should have showered this scoundrel Presto with gold instead of letting him go. Who knew?"

A melancholy Lux thought, "It seems I made a big mistake by pushing Presto away. But who could have thought?"

IT'S HER...

Once, Ellen, accompanied by Presto, Hoffman, and two other actresses pulled up to a fashionable movie theater. Performers involved in Presto's film were interested how the upper classes reacted to it. Presto had to work hard to talk Ellen into going.

In the car, Antonio, taking advantage of a lively conversation between the other two actresses and Hoffman, asked Ellen quietly, "When will you give me your answer, Ellen?"

She understood what Presto was asking her, but said nothing. Only her lips shook.

As she stepped out of the car, Ellen saw two ladies in expensive fur coats. They gazed at her with acute curiosity.

"Look! It's her – the one the newspapers wrote about! The new film star and Presto's mistress," the long-nosed lady said.

"Yes, it's her!" her plump companion agreed. They followed Ellen with unceremonious stares.

Ellen grew deathly pale, as if someone slapped her in public.

Through the entire movie, she sat motionless in the back of the box, never looking at the screen. Presto tried in vain to draw her out. Ellen's behavior was beginning to trouble him.

The audience applauded, as if the actors on screen could hear them.

"Doesn't she care about this overwhelming success?" Presto thought anxiously.

Without a single word, Ellen returned home and locked herself in her room. She couldn't hold back any longer and allowed herself to cry.

There was a knock on the door.

"It's Presto," Ellen thought. "What a bad timing. Poor man! He is waiting for my answer. But what can I tell him?"

She wiped her eyes and opened the door.

She was faced with her companion, Missis Irwin.

"Pardon me, Miss, I won't take much of your time," she said looking into Ellen's red eyes. Without waiting for an invitation she took a seat and said, "You have been crying, Miss. I can see it from your eyes."

"I wasn't hiding that," Ellen replied.

"Yes, you have something to cry about. Tears are the usual price for poorly thought-out actions and careless behavior," Missis Irwin said sanctimoniously.

"What poorly thought-out actions? What careless behavior?" Ellen asked, feeling her cheeks and her entire face turning red.

Missis Irwin looked at her mockingly.

"Please," she said sternly, "there is no need for this pretense of insulted innocence. You know very well what I am talking about."

"I assure you, I do not."

"Indeed?" Missis Irwin asked with a smile. "You must be the only person who doesn't know what all the papers are writing about, what everyone talks and shouts about on every corner in the United States."

"Do you really believe this slander?" Ellen exclaimed indignantly.

Missis Irwin shrugged.

"Why doesn't anyone write anything like that about me? There is no smoke without a fire. But, presently, the matter pertains to me and not to you. Mister Presto deceived me and offered me a very bad deal by inviting me to be your companion or, essentially to use my presence as a screen for debauchery."

"You are out of line, Missis Irwin! This conversation cannot continue!"

"Calm down. It will end soon," Missis Irwin said sternly. "Believe me, it gives me not the slightest pleasure to be talking to someone like you. I am not a kept woman. I am a poor woman, but honest. My honor and my good name are all that I have, my entire fortune. And I might lose even that by staying at this house. And so I must leave."

"The sooner you do that, the better," Ellen said, feeling that she wouldn't be able to control her temper much longer.

"Don't worry. I have already ordered to pack my things and have the car waiting."

Missis Irwin rose proudly and, without offering to shake her hand, without another glance at Ellen, swept majestically out of the room.

Ellen collapsed on the bed.

THE FINAL STRIKE

All was well. The movie was successful. The company was saved. All that was left now was to end the lonely bachelorhood.

Presto paced his study in a hopeful mood. He was waiting for Ellen to give him her answer whether she would be his wife.

Ellen was running late, and he paced faster as he grew impatient.

Finally, there was a knock on the door. Presto ran to open, intending to take his bride into his arms. He opened the door and saw Mister Barry – Ellen's uncle.

The old man was buttoned up in his coat and looked careworn and even sad.

"Mister Barry!" Presto exclaimed, unable to conceal his disappointment. "I am happy to see you. Hello. But, I must admit, I was expecting Miss Kay. She is alright, I hope?"

"She is fine," Barry replied. "But… Ellen asked me to talk to you."

Presto's mood deflated.

"Please, sit," he said in a halting voice. "Why couldn't she talk to me herself?"

They sat down.

"It would have been difficult for her. Very difficult. She loves you, sir."

"Is she refusing to be my wife?" Presto asked.

"Yes, much to my regret."

"But, my God! Why? For what reason?"

"I believe you know the reason as well as I do."

"The disgusting slander in the newspaper. But it's all over now," Presto said heatedly.

"This can never be over, Mister Presto. You know the proverb – if you throw mud, some of it will stick."

"Nothing will stick. Our marriage is the best way to get rid of the mud. Is it really worth paying attention to?"

"Listen to me, Mister Presto. Believe me, I am myself deeply saddened that your marriage is off. But I agree with Ellen. It must not happen."

"She spared you and cared about the picture, she did not want to upset you until after the last scene was shot. After all, you too tried to hide the newspaper articles from her…"

"Perhaps, she once again had doubts as to whether I was marrying her for love and not out of some noble aspirations."

"She believes in your love, as do I, and has no doubt that you are sincere. But listen, she said, 'The entire country knows about the slander. And now, everyone knows me as a movie star. The greater my fame, the higher the pedestal, the more people will point, wink, and say – it's her.' How many people tried to cover up an illicit union with marriage, but the stain remained?"

"Yes, but our relationship was completely innocent!"

"I have no doubt about that," Barry objected. "But that is the horror of all that defamation – everyone is free to believe or disbelieve."

Presto grabbed his head and exclaimed, "I think I'm going mad! Did she also decide to give up her acting career? She received right away what millions of people dream about."

"You mean fame and money?" Barry interrupted. "One's honor is more precious than that. At least, Ellen and I think so."

"I think so too," Presto replied with some displeasure. "But it's a loss to the art, to the people."

"You told me once that some nutcase asked you to keep your disfigurement, your never healing wound, for the sake of art and the people. And you told her, quite sensibly, that such demand was ridiculous and selfish."

Presto realized the truthfulness of these arguments. He was disarmed and defeated.

They gazed at each other sadly. Finally, Presto said, "What are you planning to do?"

"To go into obscurity, to go where no one knows us and live a simple and modest life. She also asked me to tell you that she sincerely wishes you happiness and that she would never forget you. I have no doubt that she will never love again, she is not that kind of girl. But her life is shattered."

Barry rose and held out his hand, shaking from agitation. "Thank you for everything, Mister Presto, and farewell."

"But can't I see her, say good bye to her?" Presto exclaimed.

"This would have been too much for her. She is already gone."

Barry left the room in the shuffling gait of a deeply suffering man.

Presto sat down onto a chair and once again squeezed his head between his hands.

Sebastian came in, sighed, waited by the door, then said, "Miss Kay is gone, and Mister Barry just asked for a cab."

"I know, Sebastian," Presto replied, still holding his head.

Sebastian didn't leave but kept waiting by the door.

"I also know what you want to ask me," Presto said. "Miss Ellen and Mister Barry are gone for good. There will be no wedding. It's just you and me once again, old man."

A long and tiresome silence filled the room. Then, as if forgetting about Sebastian's presence Presto said to himself, "But no. I am no longer alone. My enemies have dealt me a very painful blow. Well, they have only helped me define my path more clearly. No one can derail me now. I shall take revenge and fight to my last breath."

With fear and respect Sebastian watched Antonio's burning face filled with determination and rage.

ABOUT THE AUTHOR

Alexander Romanovich Belyaev was born in 1884 in Smolensk, in the family of a Russian Orthodox minister. His sister Nina and brother Vasily both died young and tragically.

Following the wishes of his father, Alexander graduated the local seminary but decided not to become a minister. On the contrary, he graduated a passionate atheist. After the seminary he entered a law school in Yaroslavl. When his father died unexpectedly, Alexander had to find ways to make ends meet including tutoring, creating theater sets and playing violin in a circus orchestra.

Fortunately, his law studies did not go to waste. As soon as Belyaev graduated the law school, he established a private practice in his home town of Smolensk and soon acquired a reputation of a talented and shrewd attorney. He took advantage of the better income to travel, acquire a very respectable art collection and create a large library. Belyaev felt so secure, financially, that he got married and left his law practice to write full-time.

At the age of thirty-five Belyaev was faced with the most serious trial of his life. He became ill with Plevritis which, after an unsuccessful treatment attempt, developed into spinal tuberculosis and leg paralysis. His wife left him, unwilling to be tied to a sick man. Belyaev spent six years in bed, three of which – in a full-torso cast. Fortunately, the other two women in his life – his mother and his old nanny – refused to give up on him. They helped seek out specialists who could help him and took him away from the dismal climate of central Russia to Yalta – a famous Black Sea resort.

While at the hospital in Yalta, Belyaev started writing poetry. He also determined that, while he could not do much with his body, he had to do something with his mind. He read all he could find by Jules Verne, H.G. Wells and by the famous Russian scientist Tsiolkovsky. He studied languages, medicine, biology, history, and technical sciences.

No one had a clear idea how, but in 1922 Belyaev finally overcame his illness and returned to normal life and work. To cut the cost of living, Belyaev moved his family from the expensive Yalta to Moscow and took up law once again. At the same time, he put all the things he learned during the long years of his illness to use, by weaving them into fascinating adventure and science fiction plots. His works appeared more and more frequently in scientific magazines, quickly earning him the title of "Soviet Jules Verne".

After successfully publishing several full-length novels, he moved his family to St. Petersburg (then Leningrad) and once again became a full-time writer. Sadly, the cold damp climate had caused a relapse in Belyaev's health. Unwilling to jeopardize his family's finances by moving to yet another resort town, he compromised by moving them somewhat further south, where the cost of living was still reasonable – to Kiev.

The family didn't get to enjoy the better climes for long. In 1930 the writer's six-year old daughter died of meningitis, his second daughter contracted rickets, and his own illness once again grew worse.

The following years were full of ups and downs. There was the meeting with one of Belyaev's heroes – H.G. Wells n 1934. There was the parting of ways with the magazine Around the World after eleven years of collaboration. There was the controversial article Cinderella about the dismal state of science fiction at the time.

Shortly before the Great Patriotic War (June 22, 1941 – May 9, 1945), Alexander Romanovich went through yet another surgery and could not evacuate when the war began. The town of Pushkin, a St. Petersburg suburb, where Belyaev and his family lived, became occupied by the German troops. Belyaev died of hunger in January, 1942. A German general and four soldiers took his body away and buried it somewhere. It was highly irregular for the members of the German military to bury a dead Soviet citizen. When asked about it the general explained that he used to enjoy Belyaev's books as a boy, and considered it his duty to bury him properly.

The exact place of Belyaev's burial is unknown to this day. After the war, the Kazan cemetery of the town of Pushkin received a commemorative stele as the sign of remembrance and respect for the great author.